Immortal Talks

Published by Seer Books Pvt. Ltd.

Copyright © Shunya 2017

The moral right of the author has been asserted

ISBN : 978-81-933052-0-1

FICTION/PHILOSOPHY

Printed and bound at Thomson Press (India) Ltd.

Prologue

It was an ordinary afternoon in the jungle except for the presence of two middle-aged men crouched behind a tree. They peered into the distance at a group of tribal people who were collecting firewood. With long, bushy hair and beards, both the men appeared to have tried their best to look like jungle dwellers. The undeceived birds, however, sat in wary silence on the branches above, as though trying to ascertain the intentions of the trespassers.

'Another day wasted,' sighed one of the men. Abandoning his stealthy posture, he slumped down, relaxing his back against the trunk of the tree. 'Hanudas, we shouldn't be afraid to conclude that there is nothing special about these people. They can't see anything we can't, and certainly not the immortal Lord Hanuman.'

'I—I suppose you are right, Swamiji,' said Hanudas, sounding resigned. He sat back and faced Swamiji so that the tribal people were still within his sight around the tree trunk. With one eye on his research subjects and another on the bushy face of his companion, his mind slipped into a long reminiscence.

He, along with Swamiji, was surreptitiously tailing a community of tribal people in his long quest to know Lord Hanuman, who was said to be one of the immortals. If he had heard the word 'Hanuman' five years ago, it would have been unintelligible to him. Even his own religion had been alien to him, except for donating to charities and offering prayers on special occasions. He had been slave to an elite lifestyle in the city of Toronto until he lost his wife in an accident, and then his only son to drugs and paranoid Schizophrenia. He had helplessly watched his son tormented by things that weren't *real* and people that didn't *exist*.

It had sucked the life out of him drop by drop, or life as he knew it at that point of time: flashing wealth to seek the approval of friends, scheming to subdue competitors, trying to keep up with every latest trend, labelling and sorting every single thing into the mental compartments of likes-dislikes and good-bad, and keeping his mind busy in mundane activities to escape from his inner self.

The day he had buried his son he became strangely hollow, like a hoop which lets things pass through it. Every experience—sounds through his ears, visuals through his eyes, and air through his nostrils—had started passing through him without leaving any trace in his mind. No sorrow. No pain. No regret. He had buried everything in the grave along with his son's body.

After the burial when his brother was driving him home, he stared blankly out the window. It was not until his eyes met an extremely unusual scene that his mind got reactivated. 'Bigfoot—magical—flying monkey...' he shouted involuntarily as he saw a giant, hairy figure flying so that it seemed to hover horizontally over a car that was running alongside theirs.

'There is no such thing there,' his brother replied ruefully. 'You need rest.' His brother had clearly thought that his son's death was causing him to go mad.

He had shot his brother a stern look of disbelief. 'Of course, there—.' He had broken off when he returned his gaze outside his car window, and the magical creature was no longer there. He had peered out to find the roof of that car completely empty, except for a small saffron flag fluttering on its front. To his utter astonishment, the flag was imprinted with a figure very much like the one he had seen hovering over the roof a moment before. That, as he later came to know, was the immortal Lord Hanuman. One of the seats in that car was occupied by a holy man, with a long beard adorning his serene face. That was the first time he had seen his Guru, or Gurudeva as he fondly calls him.

'That was no hallucination, Hanudas. You actually had a glimpse of the immortal Lord Hanuman that afternoon,' Gurudeva had explained a few months later to him. He had come to India, leaving his past identity behind in Toronto; Gurudeva had given him a new name, Hanudas—the one surrendered to Lord Hanuman. Gurudeva confirmed, 'Lord Hanuman was indeed hovering over my car, protecting me from the evil forces that see me as their enemy because I am healing misery-stricken souls all over the world.'

'I haven't even been in the slightest doubt, Gurudeva, that it was real; the most real experience I have ever had,' he replied, feeling embarrassed of the fact that he had described that incident to Gurudeva with an ample amount of doubt out of fear of being ridiculed and labelled mad. To cover his embarrassment, he hastily added, 'In fact, Gurudeva, a moment later, Lord Hanuman disappeared and all I could see was a small flag fluttering in the air. It appeared as though Lord

Hanuman had entered into that flag in the form of a small imprint. That seemed unreal to me. I think Lord Hanuman was still there in His full physical form, hovering over your car, but my eyes had lost the divine power required to see Him. My deluded eyes could now see only His small imprint on the flag.'

'Imprint on the flag, yes,' said Gurudeva with a broad smile, 'that is what ordinary human eyes see. You know, Hanudas, during the war of Mahabharata, Lord Hanuman was present, floating right over the chariot of Arjuna, doing the job assigned to Him: protecting the chariot from covert attacks. Only Pandavas and Lord Krishna could see Him there. For the eyes of enemies, he was merely an imprint on a flag hoisted on the chariot.' Gurudeva had given a short, mysterious glance at the idol of Lord Hanuman present in the room. He thought for a moment that the idol had blinked back at Gurudeva.

'Only pure souls can see Lord Hanuman,' Gurudeva further explained. 'When you were returning from your son's funeral, your mind was absolutely blank, completely free and detached from everything the external world had to offer. The moment you saw Lord Hanuman hovering over my car, your mind got reactivated and relapsed into doing what a human mind generally does. Instead of letting that divine experience pass through freely, your mind became restless to find an explanation, a label, a category that could fit the experience. It feverishly rummaged into deeper mental compartments where memories of your past experiences are stored, and perhaps came up with some labels like 'magical', 'unexplained', 'delusional', 'impossible'. Your soul got clouded by your mind's mundane little adventures and, as a result, Lord

Hanuman disappeared for you. When your soul becomes pure again, the way it was shortly after your son's funeral, you will see Him again.'

'Gurudeva, what should I do to make my soul pure again? I have already lost my family, I have nothing else to lose…if that is what it takes to purify the soul,' he asked as his mind craved sympathy, his body a warm hug.

'An aware soul is a pure soul,' replied Gurudeva plainly, ruffling the feathers of his pet parrot that had now landed on his forearm. 'If a soul is aware of who it is and where it is headed, it is pure. Are you'—Gurudeva looked in his eyes—'aware of who you are and where you are headed?'

'Yes, Gurudeva,' he replied at once. 'I just want to spend the rest of my life in your service. I have been running after mundane things all my life. Now I want to pursue the supreme truth.'

'That reply came, I am afraid, from your mind, not necessarily your soul,' said Gurudeva, sticking out his arm, and the bird took it as a cue to fly away.

Hanudas hadn't been able to find any words to reply to that.

'Hanudas, your soul, like the majority of humans of this era, is asleep,' said Gurudeva, a mysterious, faint smile on his face. 'Your soul awoke for a brief period of time on the day you buried your son. But then it slumped back into drowsiness. The alien souls have taken charge of your body and mind yet again. Earlier, your mind was making you chase materialistic pleasures, and now it is craving rest and peace in the name of a spiritual pursuit.'

At this, he had prostrated before Gurudeva and started sobbing uncontrollably. Gurudeva remained indifferent and unmoved, and instead busied himself with crooning to his pet birds. It was not until Hanudas controlled himself and sat silently and upright again that Gurudeva spoke.

'Hanudas, this fragile, crying self is not you; this is your mind. You are a powerful soul connected to the immortal Lord Hanuman, but your mind is a weak slave of the external world, Maya. There are innumerable ways Maya can control your mind, and one of them is by infiltrating alien souls into your body-mind.

'Lord Hanuman is directing your soul, your soul in turn should direct your mind, and your mind should then interact with Maya accordingly. But in your case, as in the case of millions of ignorant human beings, it has reversed: Your mind is taking directions from Maya while your soul is lulled into ignorance. Once you awaken your soul, Lord Hanuman Himself will guide your actions. He will take you wherever you need to go to fulfil your...'

Gurudeva's words had stopped registering in his mind. He sat there staring at Gurudeva, his mind absolutely blank. In a fleeting flash of divine light, he saw the path he had to follow; he realized what he had to do.

The next morning, he left Gurudeva's hermitage for no particular destination, with nothing but a backpack of essentials and most importantly, Gurudeva's blessings. He had wandered for months from glittering cities to dark remote villages, from mighty mountains to endless plains, from uninhabited caves to crowded temples, in search of nothing. He had met people from all walks of life, from sages who live alone in solitude to holy men who guide millions of their followers, in want of nothing. He had let a variety of experiences pass through his mind the way water flows between shores of a river. He didn't know whether his soul awoke or not, but he had successfully lulled his mind to sleep, a sleep so deep that no experience, no matter how painful or joyful, how dull or extraordinary, could linger in his mind, let alone instruct or control it. He could tell that Maya no longer had control of his mind, although he couldn't tell whether his soul had gained back its hold on his mind or not.

He felt a tingling in his mind after a long time when, in the course of his wanderings, he came across a group of tribal people. He had no particular reason to believe it, nonetheless, a forceful thought lingered in his mind that those people—or the Mahtangs, as he later came to call them—could see and interact with something invisible. This thought had spawned a faint hope in his mind that the invisible being they interacted with was the immortal Lord Hanuman. Where had this thought and hope come from? What was the origin? The origin couldn't be anything external since he hadn't seen anything special or different in these people that could inspire such a thought and hope. It had to be something internal, something deeper than the mind, probably the soul.

He assumed that his long wanderings had, finally, resulted in a mild current of awareness in his soul. Had he finally reached where Gurudeva, and probably Lord Hanuman, wanted him to be? Two other sages who had agreed to assist him in studying the behaviour of the Mahtangs, however, believed the contrary; they thought he had been wasting time with those jungle dwellers.

After several months of tailing the Mahtangs, all he had been able to obtain was a set of seven symbols inscribed on several things like broken clay pots, tree trunks, rocks and even on sand. Though, as he had admitted to his fellow sages, there was nothing unique about those symbols. He had seen similar, but not the same, symbols painted on huts in remote tribal villages of India. During the course of his wanderings, he had witnessed hundreds of rituals, which a judgemental mind would instantly label as superstitions, where mysterious symbols had been drawn on various objects. He never tried to find their meaning. Perhaps the people who drew them had also forgotten their original meaning if it ever existed. He learned that a ritual is all about the experience, and not about understanding. Furthermore, he had been wandering in order to lull his mind to sleep, not to activate it further by trying to grasp the meaning of every little thing.

In the case of the symbols he obtained from the Mahtangs, however, he had felt an inner urge to find the meaning. It was certainly not a usual curiosity of the mind, but an inner calling that had him tailing the Mahtangs in a faint, unclear hope.

His two fellow sages who were assisting him in this pursuit, Swamiji and Brahmachariji, had been growing uninterested as the days passed without any breakthrough. Only a few minutes ago, all three of them had tried to meet the eldest of this tribe, Baba. He had snubbed them so waspishly that Brahmachariji had called it a day. Then he and Swamiji stationed themselves behind this tree. They had been intently observing a group of tribal women, who were collecting firewood, for any unusual activity that could confirm that they could see the immortal Lord Hanuman.

The reminiscent glow in Hanudas's eyes faded and

was replaced instantly by a twinkle of hope; he had heard a commotion in the distance. The same group of tribal women stood there horror-struck as they watched one of their companions, a young, slim woman screaming and throwing punches in the air. Her body twitched and jerked violently, her extremities flailing about wildly.

'A seizure attack, perhaps. Nothing new,' mumbled Hanudas. He had seen plenty of such scenes already in a variety of settings. Every culture he had observed treated such abnormalities differently. From black magic to ghost attack, from the work of evil to blessings of deities, he had seen every possible perspective on it. Therefore, he found it hopelessly uninteresting. 'Should we call it a day, Swamiji? Let's return.'

'Let these women leave first. Then we will be able to sneak away without much effort,' replied Swamiji, sitting comfortably against the tree trunk, observing the frantic movements of a lost red ant.

As her seizure attack subsided, the tribal woman lay down under a tree. The other women in the group dispersed and busied themselves once again collecting firewood. For a fleeting moment, Hanudas had the same hollow feeling of nothingness which he'd had on the day of his son's burial. In that moment, he saw three human-like figures of light quivering near the seemingly asleep tribal woman. The next moment, he gulped in astonishment and those figures vanished. His mind assumed them to be a trick of the light.

Several minutes later, the young woman sat up and toppled forward immediately. As she sprawled her legs behind her, it looked as though she was prostrating herself before an invisible power.

His eyes couldn't see it but somehow he felt that she was prostrated before Lord Hanuman. He jerked Swamiji awake from meditation and made him aware of the development.

A minute later, the woman stood up, her palms joined against her chest. She stayed in that position for several minutes.

He felt that her lips were moving as though she was talking to someone. Swamiji, however, thought that she was standing silently, tight-lipped, as though in prayer.

'For someone who just had a violent seizure, she was behaving quite normally,' said Swamiji, trying to start a discussion, as they left the place half an hour later.

Hanudas, however, couldn't have been less interested in any discussion. He was floating in a state of thoughtlessness, beyond the boundaries of the mind. Swamiji thought it to be just another wasted day, but Hanudas knew he was just a few steps away from meeting the one his soul had been longing for.

Very soon afterwards, he deciphered the meaning of the set of seven symbols he had collected from the Mahtangs. It was a puzzle that translated as follows: 'The immortal Lord Hanuman comes every 41 years to impart supreme knowledge to his disciples, the Mahtangs.'

Over the course of the next several months, he collected thousands of such symbols, or the puzzles, wherein lay enshrined the entire knowledge Lord Hanuman imparted to His disciples. He, with the help of other sages, deciphered these puzzles and documented them under the title *Immortal Talks*.

Chapter 1
The Alternate Mother

The air was thick with conflict and confusion, a rare occurrence for a place inhabited by the disciples of Lord Hanuman, the Mahtangs. The head of Mahtangs, Baba, called a meeting of the wisest in the community to resolve the conflict overflowing between Sucheta and Vicheta, both of whom claimed to be the biological mother of Chitta.

'Divine souls, we gather here this evening to ponder about the situation of conflict which threatens to cast clouds of ignorance and illusion on our community,' said Baba, a short, thin, old man, his small face almost buried beneath the straggly white beard and long, untidy hair. 'We all know that Sucheta gave birth to Chitta about a year ago. But since the last new moon, which was just two nights ago, Vicheta has shockingly developed not only motherly feelings towards Chitta, but also memories that she had given birth to Chitta. As if this confusion was not enough, Chitta's feelings towards his real mother, Sucheta, have run dry, and he now identifies Vicheta as his mother. Sucheta suspects that Vicheta has performed some kind of black magic to steal her son. Since Vicheta is childless, she has the motive to commit this crime, believes Sucheta.'

At Baba's last two sentences, Vicheta, who was sitting there anxiously as Chitta snuggled in her bosom, broke into irrepressible sobs, tears streaming down from her reddened eyes.

Baba, as an old man who had seen all kinds of emotions masked and unmasked, knew that Vicheta had not committed any wrong purposefully. However, the high seat he occupied didn't allow him to draw conclusions based on his feelings.

'Vicheta, I am afraid your tears can't prove your innocence,' continued Baba ruthlessly, bringing more stiffness to his voice than he intended. 'All Mahtangs who walk the path of highest truth, the birds and animals that are our companions, all directions which register every action we perform in this mortal world, the air we breathe, the light which reveals this world to us, and every particle of this mortal world are witness to the fact that Sucheta gave birth to Chitta from her womb. We have all seen her bringing up Chitta. Until two days back she could be seen feeding Chitta her milk.

'What magic have you done so that now Chitta doesn't get off your lap? How can you snatch away someone's child like this? Remember, Lord Hanuman is, though not visible here right now, watching everything. Do not commit such a sin, Vicheta. Before the laws of mother nature set punishment for you, which shall be very harsh I warn you, withdraw your black magic and let Chitta go to Sucheta, his real mother.'

Even though everyone agreed with every word Baba said, it sounded very harsh against the backdrop of Vicheta's increasingly hysterical sobs. Baba's wife Mata, who was sitting alongside him, shot him a reproachful look, got down from her high seat, sat down on the ground next to Vicheta and flung her arm around her shoulders consolingly.

'I am telling the truth. ...' uttered Vicheta, her sobs getting softer, with the back of her head nestled in Mata's arm. 'I gave birth to Chitta. ... I have been feeding him with my milk since his first cry. ... I have protected him from the dangers of the jungle. ... You are my family; how can you turn so against me? Mata, you were present when I gave birth to Chitta, weren't you? How could you forget that? ... And Baba, you were the one who performed the rituals on the seventh day of his birth. ... You were present when Chitta was given the first bath. ... How could you erase that from your memory, Baba? How could you? I have never seen Chitta in Sucheta's arms. Then why do you all assert that Sucheta had been taking care of Chitta until a couple of days ago?'

'Oh yes, everyone except you is deluded,' snarled Sucheta. 'Come back to your senses, you pathetic creature! Give me my son back.'

'Come to think of it,' said Baba Mahtang, 'the likelihood of Vicheta alone being deluded can't be more than that of the rest of us being deluded. It is possible that somehow all of our memories have been altered so that we all remember Sucheta as Chitta's mother while Vicheta—'

'But how?' Mata cut across Baba, 'which evil power in the universe would dare do that given that mighty Lord Hanuman is guarding us?'

'Assuming that we all are inside a delusion created by an evil power, there is no point in discussing this matter further. Doing so would mean playing by the rules of the delusion. We need a neutral, unaffected, third party who can see through the delusion,' said Baba, looking up at the

Sun sinking towards the westward hills. Vicheta's sobs had subsided into hiccoughs at this argument of Baba's.

'No,' interrupted Sucheta, 'I am not deluded. Vicheta is. I am Chitta's real mother, Baba.'

'A deluded person would also say the same,' said Baba politely. 'You need to know the light in order to recognize the darkness you dwell in; else you would mistake the darkness for the light. Well, as I said, there is no point of discussion. I am going to consult our ancestors who live along the negative coordinates of Time. I am sure they can look more objectively at this matter and point to where we have erred. The Sun is sinking, the day is almost through, the night, which is the most suitable time to connect with our ancestors, will fall soon. I'd better hurry and reach the hilltop.'

'Can I...' uttered Sucheta hesitatingly, 'Baba, I am horrified at the thought that I could be deluded. Can I accompany you to the hilltop so that I...?'

'Alright,' said Baba. 'But if you are coming with me, Vicheta ought to come too. You are both equal to me. ... Yes, you can bring Chitta also,' he added at Vicheta's enquiring look.

After about two hours of a tiring but hopeful journey, they reached the bottom of the topmost cliff—the Ancestors' cliff. As Mahtangs visited it very often, mostly at night, they had carved a loop in its top edge so that they could easily hook a rope, even in pitch dark, and climb it. That evening, however, even as Baba threw one end of the rope up in the air, the part of it that was supposed to stay in his hands slipped away into the darkness. Assuming that one end got hooked successfully at the top, he flailed his hands frantically through the air to search for the supposedly hanging rope.

Ten minutes later, as they sat huddled on the ledge, disappointed and half thinking of returning back, Baba noticed the rope dangling right before his eyes. He grabbed it at once, tugged with all his force to check that it was safe, and started climbing up. He noticed that the rope was unusually soft but not slippery; he climbed up fast like a squirrel scurrying up a tree.

It was not until he reached the cliff top and gulped a lungful of fresh air that he realized the rope was not hooked in the loop where he imagined it to be; it stretched well beyond the edge onto the surface of the cliff top. Curious to find the end of the rope, he peered into the darkness and saw a figure whom he immediately recognized as the immortal Lord Hanuman.

The thing he tugged to climb up the cliff was not a rope but the tail of Lord Hanuman who was sitting in the middle of the cliff top, a sphere of white light creating a magical halo around His head, His bright smile dissolving darkness around Him into a reddish-gold glow.

Baba couldn't have asked for anything more. He had come to speak to his ancestors and got to meet the Guru of all his ancestors.

His jaw dropped and eyes widened at the heavenly sight of his immortal Guru. A minute later, he couldn't feel his body. All he could feel of himself was a speck of light floating mid-air. Lord Hanuman, however, saw that Baba's body shook feverishly on the spot for a minute, then sprawled onto the ground and started rolling around, circling Him like a moth circles a light.

One could never predict how a mortal body would behave around the immortal.

After several minutes of insane movements, Baba's body prostrated full length and stock-still before Lord Hanuman, tears streaming from his eyes.

'Stand up, Baba. Get on to your feet,' said Lord Hanuman, bending down to reach Baba's shoulders.

Baba stood up and gathered his bearings for a moment—Sucheta, Vicheta and Chitta had also reached—and bowed his head in reverence before Lord Hanuman.

In the silence that ensued, Baba thought how the conflict of Sucheta-Vicheta had made him and his fellow Mahtangs forget they were expecting Lord Hanuman's arrival for several months now. His body was feeling extremely light as though it had just shed a ton of impurities. He was having this enlightening feeling for the first time since Lord Hanuman left them 41 years ago with the eternal promise of coming back after four decades.

'Welcome back to this land of mortals, Deva,' said Baba with the air of a host welcoming their guest at the door. 'I, on behalf of the entire Mahtang community, express my gratitude. I can't thank you enough for coming to—'

'Well, I thought you came to me, and not the other way around,' said Lord Hanuman in a booming voice, a broad smile on his serene face.

Baba realized that Lord Hanuman had already started His lessons; yes, technically they had come to Lord Hanuman through the path of austerities performed for the last 41 years. Those who didn't take that path wouldn't be able to see Him, even if they stood right before Him.

'Yes, Deva, I have come to you,' said Baba, 'whichever way I think about it. I came here to this cliff to find a solution to Chitta's problem.'

'Chitta is happy, isn't he?' said Lord Hanuman, turning his attention to Vicheta who was clutching Chitta tightly to her. 'Yes, he is perfectly happy in the arms of his mother.'

'But, Deva, Sucheta is his real mother,' said Baba, feeling slightly relieved that after Lord Hanuman's arrival he was no longer the topmost man in his community.

'Well, Baba, we can't determine it for Chitta. He knows best who his mother is.'

'He is just a small child, Deva. How can we leave this decision to him? He could be easily drawn into delusion by black magic,' said Baba, trying hard to hide a note of exasperation from his voice.

'Just a small child?' said Lord Hanuman, whipping His tail up in the air. 'Look at my tail, Baba. For something that brought you up this cliff, doesn't it look very small?'

'Forgive me, Deva,' mumbled Baba realizing his ignorance at once. 'Chitta is not just a small child. He is a soul which has experienced numerous births before. That makes him as old as anyone else on this cliff. But what I meant to say was that he...'

Baba got distracted by the loud and hysterical giggles of Chitta. Apparently, Chitta's eyes had caught sight of Lord Hanuman's tail, which was expanding and shrinking funnily. Lord Hanuman too allowed Himself a soft chuckle.

The notes of hysteria in Chitta's giggles soon turned into distinct words. Baba thought his mind had just learned a new language: the language of baby giggles.

'I was a monk,' said Chitta, apparently recounting his previous birth in the language of baby giggles. 'I was wandering in search of God, where else but in the land of Hindus, India.

'In my earnest quest to find the supreme truth, I happily lost track of time and space. Once, a deadly thirst pulled me to my senses and I realized that I was walking barefoot on a deserted country lane that was surrounded by open crop fields on both sides. It was a very hot summer afternoon. The earth I was staggering on was hot enough to cook a meal. My body had lost its every drop of water before it managed to send an alarm signal to my *dead* mind.

'My immediate response was to take it as a new level of challenge set against me by Maya and an opportunity for me to show my spiritual strength. For some reason, however, I thought better of it and started looking for water which my body so desperately needed. I looked around. There was no sign of a human presence as far as my eyes could see and my hope could show. One option was to go deep inside the fields and look for a water container farmers might have kept for their use. Another option was to reach the nearest village along the lane. I went ahead with the latter; my mind argued that if I collapsed, there were better chances of being found by someone on the main lane than in the fields.

'Mercifully, there was a house situated in the uninhabited outskirts of the village I had aimed to reach. It was just a hut built of mud bricks and thatched with grass, fronted by a small courtyard fully shadowed by a single tree.

'A child was lying on a charpoy under the tree, apparently counting the leaves. "Child, can I please get a glass of water?" I asked, feeling sorry to have trespassed into his world of imagination.

'The child immediately leapt to his feet and went inside the hut to fetch water. I followed him up to the door in my desperate hurry to thrust water onto my lips immediately when he brought it. But a scene of horrific misery was waiting there to kill my thirst.

'I heard weak, pained groans emanating from a corner of that dark, sweltering, and musty hovel. As my eyes adjusted to the darkness, I saw a frail, physically drained woman lying with her mouth open. Every part of her body was lifeless, except her throat which grumbled continuously in agony. "What... what happened?" I uttered hoarsely, my throat choking out of compassion.

'The woman tried to lift her eyelids but couldn't manage it. I turned to the boy who stood beside the water pot. Clearing my throat, I posed the same question to him, "What happened to your mother, child?"

'He didn't answer and dropped his gaze down to the cup of water he was holding for me.

'For someone who was dying of thirst a few moments ago, it was quite inexplicable to have found that cup of water an eyesore. My mind had, by sheer nature, chased away thirst and occupied itself with a more painful experience.

'I knelt down to look into the eyes of the child, put the cup of water back to the pitcher and said, "Maybe I can cure your mother. Tell me exactly what happened to her."

'As the boy responded with a blank look, I asked an easier question, "Where is your father, child?"

'Since the boy didn't answer, I looked around to get some clues. I saw a poster of Lord Hanuman hanging on the wall overlooking the ailing woman's charpoy. The poster appeared to be a bit grimy. An unlit squalid lamp stood on a makeshift table reasonably away from the wall. Beside the lamp lay some strips of tablets.

'Every single object that was present under that thatched roof seemed to be an embodiment of wretchedness except the poster of Lord Hanuman, where my eyes found rest and my mind reassurance; I fixed my gaze on it and forgot the scene of misery surrounding me.

'After a moment, or that is what it felt like, I was brought back to the misery by the entry of two men, one of them the boy's father and the other, I assumed, a charlatan doctor. As the charlatan got busy injecting tranquilizers to relieve the patient's pain, I looked enquiringly at the other man.

'Having stared warily into my rugged face for a while, he cast his eyes around to check that the boy was no longer in the hut and muttered, "On her deathbed... long, incurable disease..."

'I shouted indignantly, "Incurable? Just because this ignorant charlatan says so? Take her to a hospital, you deplorable man!"

'The charlatan turned around and said rather patiently, "It's cancer, advanced stages. All the doctors he could afford have pronounced her incurable. I am just easing her pain by injecting painkillers."

'At a complete loss of what to do, I stormed out of the hovel, though not before I had shot a final complaintive look at the poster of Lord Hanuman.

'I couldn't walk past the boy who lay outside once more under the tree, lost in his own thoughts. The guilt of helplessness oozed out of me in the form of compassionate love. I sat down on the edge of his charpoy and started ruffling his hair.

'I could understand the mental turmoil the child was going through. His silence felt like an unbearable burden on my own soul; it indeed was more tumultuous than the wrath of the gods.

'In an attempt to have him speak a word or two, I said, "No school today, eh?"

'He didn't so much as twitch an eyebrow.

'I clenched my jaws, fighting to control the outburst of compassion. As I gently stroked his hair, I noticed a burn mark on his right hand.

'With a smile pulled with difficulty, I made another attempt to strike up a conversation, "Been playing with firecrackers, have you?"

'He lifted his hand to ascertain what I was talking about and mumbled, "Oh, this… it happened while cooking food."

'A child who deserved to have his mother feeding him with her hands was compelled by the circumstances to cook food. I couldn't control my emotions any longer. I clambered to my feet and staggered towards the lane whence I had come, attempting to direct all my anger and emotions towards Lord Hanuman. How could He let His devotees suffer like this?

'I had barely reached the lane when my dehydrated body gave up and collapsed, unconscious.

'When I came back to my senses, I found myself on a charpoy under a tree. The woman who was on her deathbed a short while ago was sitting crouched on the ground beside me, her one arm resting on the side of the charpoy. Surprisingly, she was looking quite healthy. Her husband supported my neck as I attempted to sit up to be able to sip water.

'Was it a dream?

'I couldn't keep my suspicions to myself. Turning my head slowly towards the man, I said, "Your... your wife was on her... her deathbed a few minutes ago... you said it was an incurable disease..."

'He exchanged a look of dreadful incredulity with his wife, apparently not able to relate to my words. I pressed on, "Yes, I was in your hut a while ago. I asked for water from your son and then I went inside to find your wife in a horrendous state of misery."

'What they took as mysterious talk of a holy man could well have been labelled utterances of an insane tramp if it weren't for my holy robes and unmistakable glow of divinity on my face.

'With hands folded in respectful salutation, the man said, "O monk, I and my wife are poor labourers. When we work nearby, we usually come to have lunch at home. We saw you collapsing when we were coming for today's lunch. We have never seen you before. How do you know that we have a son?"

'The woman's motherly instincts registered something eerie even as her husband posed this question to me. She immediately called out her son's name loudly.

'The child came running out of the hut, holding a piece of bread and onion in his hand, chewing hastily on the bite that was still in his mouth. Shockingly, he refused to recognize my face.

'Something was amiss. It got my mind buzzing in alarm. I sprang to my feet, shot the innocent family a look of suspicion and uttered hysterically, "I had come to your house a while ago. ... I can prove it. Oh, yes, I can. ... There is a burn mark on your son's hand. He told me he got it when he was cooking food. ..."

'At this, the woman, who was crouched and rooted to the spot, clutched her son tightly with both her arms. Her eyes dilated in terror, she said imploringly, "Don't do this to us, please. He is my only son. Why would I let him cook food when I am there? Yes, there is a burn mark... but that is because he touched a hot vessel accidentally. ... Don't take away my son. Please... I beg of you. ..."

'The woman probably thought that I was laying ground to initiate their son into monkhood and that I would take him with me.

'In order to disabuse her of this misunderstanding, I hastily added, "No, No... I said that to prove I was here. Furthermore, I have in my mind the full picture of the interior of your hut. I can tell the exact location of each of your possessions. ... There is a poster of Lord Hanuman on the wall. ... There is a lamp placed on—"

'I broke off as the woman scrambled up to me, dragging her son along and fell at my feet, beseechingly, pulling down the confused child into doing the same, and inspiring her dumbstruck husband to follow the course.

'It was not unusual for people to fall at my feet, swayed by the enigma of monkhood that I carried. But this was different. I despised myself for scaring, though unintentionally, a family into submission. I immediately turned around and shuffled my way towards the main lane, the imploring voices of the mother following me, "O monk, as someone who can see our past, present, and future, please don't be wrathful with us. ... forgive us if..."

'With a guilt-stricken heart and puzzled mind, I gained the main lane and trudged on towards the village.

'As the brick houses came into view on the right side, I turned my gaze left where sat a small pond, obviously soothing to the senses of someone who had collapsed a short while ago due to dehydration. Cows were relaxing in the shallow water, watched over by young boys who were frolicking in the water to beat the heat. I decided to relax under a banyan tree that offered the best view of the pond.

'The cool breeze wafting off the pond drifted me into a meditative sleep and I found myself in dream-like surroundings: There was a tree of light under which I stood aloft, having a weightless body of divine light; the landscape before me was hazy, bisected by two tunnels, one lit with red light and the other with green.

'I had a pre-conceived thought that I was in some sort of dream and I had to choose one of the tunnels to wake back into reality. As I swam up to the entrance of the red tunnel, a voice emerged from behind, "O soul, after years of rigorous austerity, you have earned yourself the ability to choose between the realities you want to live. You shall awake into a different reality depending on the tunnel you choose to use."

'I contemplated on each word that reached me but didn't think of turning around to know the source of the voice. Instead, I moved ahead and entered the red tunnel.

'The inner surface of the tunnel was like a white screen on which three dimensional visuals were projected. They appeared so real that I felt a part of them. I saw a thirsty monk tramping along a country lane. I knew that the monk was no one else but me, although I was delightfully detached from everything that was happening to him. I even had the freewill to fast forward and backward along the tunnel to see future and past life events of the monk.

'I sped forward and saw the monk entering a hovel to get water; he saw a woman on her deathbed; he felt terrible pain to see the family in such a dreadful condition; he exchanged words with the woman's husband, her son and a charlatan; he returned to the main lane without drinking water; he fainted as he turned onto the main lane; he was attended by a young man passing by (who seemed to have no connection with the woman and her family) and given water; he resumed his wanderings and reached the bank of the village pond; and lastly, he fell asleep while cursing himself for not being able to help the dying woman and gods for making a poor family suffer so terribly.

'The same voice echoed from behind, "O soul, you may exit through this tunnel if you wish to continue with the reality you just saw. As soon as you do that, you will find yourself under that banyan tree overlooking the pond. Of course, if I may point it out, not so far away from that pond there is a hovel in which the woman is still on her deathbed. If you don't want to live this reality, you may turn back and choose the green tunnel instead."

'How could I choose to live in a reality where a poor woman was about to die and I had to live with the guilt of not being able to help her? I turned back. I could see the same events happening in reverse as I floated back towards the entrance of the tunnel.

'In the middle of the red tunnel, I paused at the sight of what looked like a gateway to the adjoining green tunnel. "O soul, it is a secret gateway to the green tunnel and you have the freewill to choose this gateway," the voice echoed yet again. "However, I must warn you, a lateral entry into the green tunnel may leave you baffled. As you can see, the red tunnel represents a reality where the woman is on her deathbed and eventually dies. On the other hand, the green tunnel represents a reality where the woman had never been on her deathbed. Entering laterally from red to green will result in a paradox which will leave you completely flummoxed."

'Before heading to the secret gateway, I pored over the visuals cast on that point of the red tunnel. The monk could be seen lying unconscious on the deserted main lane a short distance away from the hovel where the woman was battling for life.

'After entering the green tunnel, the first thing I noticed was that the green light was streaked with red light which was seeping through the secret gateway from the red tunnel.

'In the green tunnel, I saw visuals of the monk lying unconscious. The woman who was on her deathbed in the red tunnel was completely healthy here. She could be seen returning back to her home for a lunch break along with her husband.

'I drifted towards the exit of the green tunnel, watching the visuals on the way. I saw that the monk was brought back to consciousness by a woman and her husband; he recalled that the woman had been on her deathbed before he fainted; the woman and her husband told him that they were returning back from work for a lunch break and that they couldn't relate to what he was talking about; he left the place in a state of puzzlement; and lastly, he reached the village pond and fell asleep.

'The voice rang yet again, "You may exit through this tunnel if you wish to continue with this reality. When you do so, you will wake up under the banyan tree overlooking the village pond. In this reality, the woman is healthy, her family is happy but you are puzzled to the point of insanity because of the paradox arising from your lateral entry from the red to green tunnel: The woman was on her deathbed before you fainted but when you came back to your senses, she was not only perfectly healthy, but also devoid of any memory or sign of any recent ailment."

'I didn't choose that reality. I turned back to explore a better option.

'The voice suggested, "Instead of making a lateral entry from the red to the green tunnel, enter the green tunnel through its main entrance. That way, the effects of the red tunnel won't leak into the green tunnel and you won't face any paradox."

'I did exactly what the voice suggested. When I entered the green tunnel through its main entrance, I noticed that it was lit in pure green light without any streak of red. The visuals projected on the inner surface of the tunnel were significantly different now: The monk came staggering in need of drinking water; before he could turn towards the hut, he collapsed on the main lane; the woman and her husband returning to their hut for a lunch break noticed him and moved him under the tree in their yard where he awoke and drank water; he thanked the couple for their kind help and resumed his wanderings; and lastly he reached the village pond and fell asleep under a banyan tree.

'When I reached the edge of the green tunnel, the voice said, "You may exit now if you want to continue with this reality. You will awake under the banyan tree in an ordinary day. No woman on her deathbed. No paradox of any kind."

'Even though this choice seemed best, I didn't choose it. I turned back, crossed the tunnel and came out of its entrance gate.

'There I stood once again under the tree of light facing a hazy landscape bisected by two clear tunnels. The voice warbled from behind me, "O soul, you need to choose one of the tunnels to wake into reality. Which tunnel do you choose?"

'I replied at once, "I choose none. They are both illusions. None is better than the other."

'The voice asserted, "They seem illusions to you because you have the freewill to choose one of them. Once you have made your choice and entered one of them, it is a reality. A hard reality where you have to actually live through pains and pleasures."

'I said firmly, "I seek freedom from pains and pleasures. I seek freedom from the cycle of birth and death. In short, I seek Moksha."

'The voice asked me to turn around. I obliged and learned that it was the voice of Lord Hanuman who stood there with His hand outstretched. He held my hand and the next thing I knew, I was born in Mahtang community as Chitta. ...'

Chitta's giggles subsided. There was a minute of silence which allowed Baba, Sucheta, and Vicheta to absorb the story of Chitta's previous birth they had just heard.

Lord Hanuman completed the story, 'That afternoon, the villagers found the dead body of a monk at the bank of the village pond. That was the end of Chitta's previous life.'

'But the paradox continues for Chitta in his present birth, as he is confused as to who his actual mother is,' Baba sighed. A sudden realization dawned on him. He glanced up at Lord Hanuman and added, 'And I wish this paradox to continue. It is such a good reminder of the illusionary nature of the mortal world we tend to passionately attach to.'

Lord Hanuman simply smiled and Sucheta took it as His approval of Baba's statement. She let out a shriek of horror as though she had been sentenced to death.

'As I said at the beginning,' Lord Hanuman said placidly, 'no one has the right to decide for Chitta. It has to be entirely on Chitta as to whom he embraces as his mother. Two days ago on the new moon, his soul had an encounter with me. I showed him seven tunnels, or the realities he could opt to enter.

'In the first reality, Sucheta is his mother and Vicheta holds no motherly feelings for him.

'In the second reality, again, Sucheta is his mother but Vicheta has painful one-sided motherly feelings for him.

'In the third reality, Vicheta is his mother and Sucheta holds no motherly feelings for him.

'In the fourth reality, Vicheta is his mother but Sucheta has painful one-sided motherly feelings for him.

'The fifth reality is a blend of the first and third, whereby Sucheta and Vicheta become his mother alternately for a fortnight. There is no conflict because when one is the mother, the other has no motherly feelings for Chitta.

'The sixth reality is a blend of the second and fourth, whereby, again, Sucheta and Vicheta become his mother alternately for a fortnight. There is conflict because when one is the mother the other has painful one-sided motherly feelings for Chitta.

'In the seventh reality, he is an abandoned child as neither Sucheta nor Vicheta have motherly feelings for him.

'His soul chose the sixth reality as it stands as a good reminder of the illusionary nature of this world which would help him attain Moksha.'

The relief that her son hadn't been stolen and the hope that Chitta would play with her again the next fortnight cheered Sucheta up a bit.

This explanation from Lord Hanuman washed away all the ill feelings between Sucheta and Vicheta and they seemed to accept the reality that they both would be Chitta's mothers alternately for rest of their lives.

Chapter 2
The Mermaid

Baba was sitting on a ledge right at the base of the Ancestors' Cliff, stunned by the surreal turn of events he had just witnessed. He went there to speak to his ancestors, but instead he got to meet—and his conscious self was still finding it too good to be real—the immortal Lord Hanuman.

The thought that Lord Hanuman was still up there on the top of the cliff was sending intermittent chills of ecstasy through his body. A part of him wanted to stay there all night in close proximity to his immortal Guru, while the rest of him wanted to rush to his hamlet and join the celebrations with his fellow Mahtangs. He had already sent Sucheta and Vicheta ahead of him carrying this paradisiacal tiding.

All the Mahtangs respected Baba next to the gods. How would he look dancing dementedly with them in ecstasy? If he were to go to the hamlet tonight, he ought to comport himself as though the arrival of Lord Hanuman were a casual affair. He must drain all his euphoria before he showed his face to the people who could never imagine him as anything but an expressionless, contemplative, wise old man.

Unable to so much as slow down the flow of excitement rushing to his head, he was about to decide on staying there overnight when a stroke of rationality hit him. Lord Hanuman hadn't indicated in any way that he would stay on the cliff overnight. What if He had left the cliff and already reached the hamlet? Being immortal, He doesn't need His feet to travel a distance. He can make His body disappear in one place and reappear instantly in another.

He leapt to his feet at once and trotted his way down the hill towards his hamlet, feverishly imagining everything that would take place for the next several days while Lord Hanuman was with them. For a man who always lived in the present moment, dwelling neither in memories of the past nor in expectations of the future, it was like a tsunami raging inside his head.

Mahtangs would be rolling, jumping, dancing, singing and expressing their exuberance in every possible way around a bonfire. Or would they be sitting quietly around the almighty Lord Hanuman who had perhaps already reached there and was telling them stories of how he spent the last 41 years?

'Oh, but I can't afford to spend time in celebrations for I must get immediately on to preparations for the grand Charna ceremony which will go on continuously for the next several days,' thought Baba. 'Would my soul depart for its true abode during one of the sessions of the Charna ceremony? Or do I have to carry on in this onerous human life for some more time?'

Baba's mind wandered through thickets of imagination all the way back as he walked, and slipped into a deep ditch of sudden shock as he reached the hamlet and found everyone asleep, except for a thin old woman with grey hair whom he immediately recognized as his wife. She was gazing into the dying embers of a fire outside their hut.

'Haven't Sucheta and Vicheta reached here yet?' asked Baba, worried. There was no sign of their presence as far as his eyes could pierce through the darkness.

'They have,' replied Mata, placing dry grass and twigs to rekindle the fire. 'They came and broke into tears—both of them—and left without speaking a word. So, the ancestors too couldn't resolve the conflict between them, eh?' said Mata as she bent low to blow on the kindling.

'What? They didn't inform you about the arrival of the immortal Lord Hanuman?' shouted Baba.

Apparently, Mata didn't hear anything. Having brought the freshly placed fuel to flames, she set a small blackened vessel of water on the fire.

'I can't believe it,' shouted Baba in exasperation. 'Mata, did you not hear what I just said? Lord Hanuman has arrived.'

'Hear what, Baba?' asked Mata, looking up. 'Why do you sound so stressed? If the conflict couldn't be resolved by the ancestors, some other way shall be found.'

Baba squatted down so that he was level with Mata's face, and said in what he meant to be a muffled shout, stressing each word, 'Lord... Hanuman... has... arrived...'

Even a deaf person could have figured out Baba's words from the clear movement of his lips, but somehow Mata didn't. While Baba shouted his lungs out, Mata saw him merely straining his face awkwardly. The words that Baba spoke and the movements he made with his lips weren't communicated to Mata. Something was amiss between the speaker and the listener, the messenger and the receptor, the seen and the seer.

After some trial and error with different tones and messages, Baba realized that Mata perfectly heard all sentences except the ones that carried information of Lord Hanuman's arrival. His heart swelled with the agony of not being able to share the happiest news of his life as head of Mahtangs. Tears rolled down his cheeks.

Mata had seen Sucheta and Vicheta break down in a similar fashion a short while earlier. She reached over to Baba around the fire, crouched beside him, flung an arm around his shoulder and started consoling him. It was extremely rare to see tears in Baba's eyes, even rarer than conflict in their community. Thinking that Baba's agony was about the nasty and presumably unresolved conflict between the two mothers, she tenderly said, 'Don't worry, Baba. We will find a way to resolve this.'

Wiping his tears with the back of his hand, Baba slumped down to the ground and took a deep breath. Realizing at once that her husband needed emotional space to pull himself together, Mata removed her arm from his shoulder and started to fidget confusedly with the burning twigs.

While the fire heated up the water, Baba's intellect cooled his mind down. By the time he washed his feet and face with the warm water, the waves of emotions that pounded his heart had subsided and he was able to think clearly again.

'Mata, suppose I wanted to convey a message to you but somehow it wouldn't reach you,' said Baba vaguely.

'Hmmm,' mumbled Mata, feigning a yawn that plainly discouraged the idea of starting a heavy conversation at this hour.

Baba removed his gaze from the fire for a second and looked at Mata, smiling. He admired this quality in his wife immensely, which he totally lacked. Despite being the chieftain's wife and one of the eldest and wisest in the community, she never encumbered herself when it came to expressing how she truly felt.

'Yes, it's too late. We should go to sleep,' said Baba, though sleep was the last thing on his mind despite being physically tired and emotionally choked.

'Yes, we should. And your desire to go to sleep has reached me plain and clear, if that was what you wanted to convey,' said Mata, rubbing her eyes wearily and standing up to leave. 'Have a nice journey to the dream world.'

'Well, you would never know what I wanted to convey until your mind was ready to receive it,' murmured Baba, unaware that Mata had already left. Apparently, he hadn't heard Mata's last sentence—have a nice journey to the dream world—in which she conveyed her goodnight wish, just as Mata hadn't heard any of his sentences in which he wanted to tell her about Lord Hanuman's arrival.

Even though his ears were open, he didn't hear Mata's goodnight wish because his mind had occupied itself with something else. Had he noticed this lapse of his own mind and ruminated on its cause, he would have progressed further in his pursuit to determine why Mata's mind was not receptive to information about Lord Hanuman's arrival.

A typical human mind remains under control of the external world, Maya, which has a never-ending arsenal of highs-lows, good-bad, right-wrong, love-hate, pleasure-pain, likes-dislikes, pure-impure, spiritual-materialistic, belief-disbelief, rational-irrational, and so on to keep a mind engaged. Therefore, Maya has all the powers to enslave a human mind and control what information the latter receives.

But there was no way Maya could have influenced the mind of Mata or that of any Mahtang for that matter. Being disciples of Lord Hanuman, their minds and souls are surrendered to Him. If anybody could control what information their minds received and ignored, it was Lord Hanuman.

Baba, however, wasn't thinking along these lines. Sitting by the crackling fire, his mind instead dived into esoteric depths of wisdom where doubts are valued more than assertions. He began to doubt the idea that he had met Lord Hanuman on the Ancestors' Cliff. It could very well have been a delusion, a hallucination induced by the mental stress he endured dealing with the conflict between Sucheta and Vicheta. A hallucination in which Sucheta, Vicheta, and Chitta were present alongside him. A mutual hallucination.

Had he succeeded in telling Mata and other Mahtangs about this, he would have assumed it to be a reality. Although, a thought would have still crossed his mind, terming it a broader hallucination mutually shared by his entire community.

The upshot of this thinking was that by the time Baba went to bed, his excitement had vanished. He took it as just another night and boarded the vehicle of sleep which transported him to the dream world.

His dreams, however, weren't significant enough to leave any trace of memory in his conscious mind, for he was an old man with no desire left except to hand over the responsibilities of Mahtang Chieftain to his successor and leave the mortal world to merge with the supreme.

Curiously enough, Mahtangs had chosen a young man called Urva, who was in his early twenties now, as the successor of Baba. Physical age never matters for Mahtangs as they regard each other as ancient souls. Any Mahtang will proudly tell how the gods had sent clear signals for them to identify their next chieftain. One of the signals was tormenting nightmares that haunted Urva since childhood.

While Baba was enjoying a peaceful sleep, Urva was being pulled into one of his haunting nightmares. In this particular nightmare, he sat crouched on the edge of a rock outcrop in the middle of the ocean with his body exhausted, heart dejected and mind numb. He didn't remember how he ended up there; all he knew was that he was lost. The hope of crossing the ocean and reaching home had also abandoned him. As the red sun sank below the horizon, he could see the face of Death staring at him from the sky.

'I will help you if you help me,' said an ambrosial voice which made him look down the edge of the rock. A girl of breath-taking beauty stood in the water below, her bright green eyes staring out of her smooth, round face.

Predisposed to thoughts of danger and death, Urva reacted as though he had spotted a lion behind a bush. He scrambled a long way up the rock before shouting, 'How— who—what do you want?'

'I can help you reach the place where the passing boats can spot you,' said the muffled voice of the girl.

Urva didn't say anything. He waited until the silence

screamed of a lost opportunity, then crept back to the lower edge of the rock which he had abandoned a minute earlier. He couldn't gather the courage to look down the rock. To check if the girl was still there, he uttered tentatively, 'Who are you?'

'An unfortunate soul trapped in the depths of the ocean. Waiting to be rescued, just like you,' the reply came in a sad voice, followed by a sigh which Urva took as a little sob.

He couldn't help but look at the source of the sob. Pressing his hands against the edge of the rock, he stuck his head out and looked down below. His eyes met the innocent misty green eyes of the girl and all his apprehensions about her dissipated at once.

'Come on up,' said Urva, lying himself flat on his belly and extending his hand to help her up.

Her soft palm strongly gripped his, and he applied a gentle upward force. She didn't rise even an inch above the water's surface. Instead, she slowly slithered further down. Thinking she was being pulled down by a predator, he summoned all his force to save her.

The thought of his own safety didn't cross his mind until he hung miraculously like a bat with only his feet glued somehow to the edge of the rock. It was too late to recoil. The giant mouth of the ocean was waiting to swallow him.

He kicked and flailed his limbs in panic as he fell rapidly through the watery depths. Unable to hold his breath any longer, he inhaled a huge amount of water. It felt like a multi-armed monster attempting to burst through his body from the inside. And then suddenly, without any effort on his part, the monster who was thrashing within him seemed to turn into vapours and came slinking out through his nostrils.

He could breathe normally again, but he was breathing water not air. He was moving through the water as though flying through the air. He looked around to see the girl flying by his side, her hand on his back dictating the directions of the flight.

The girl stared at him blankly when he shot her an enquiring look. Before his mind could be fooled again by the innocence and beauty of that face, his eyes slid over to the back of her body and he realized that it wasn't a girl, it was a mermaid. His mind immediately worked out the rest of the puzzle.

A second later, when he looked back and realized that he too had acquired a fish-like lower body, everything seemed to fit into the story suggested by his mind. He had been lured into becoming a merman.

'No,' he let out a hysterical shout, 'You can't do this to me! No.'

The mermaid's face remained largely expressionless except for a muscle or two that twitched when she pressed her hand harder against Urva's back as he tried to jerk away.

Even after forcing her prey into submission, the mermaid didn't look happy. When she reached the palace of her queen along with her quarry, she said rather glumly with her head bowed, 'O queen, please accept my contribution to the glorious heritage I am proud to be a part of.'

Urva kept glowering at the mermaid as she took the permission of the queen and floated across the room towards the exit. Just before her tail disappeared through the door, Urva shouted angrily, 'You are a liar. Cheater. You cheated me.'

Within a few hours, he had largely made peace with his new identity as a merman. He was alive at least. It was better than dying of thirst in the middle of the ocean. He was rewarded with ownership of a luxurious palace in the kingdom. As he lay in his bedroom, which was dazzling with pearls and decorated with colourful gems, he thought of his family who lived in a hut across the ocean. He realized that his desire to reach home had diminished significantly.

Memories of his family had become so dull and unexciting that his mind preferred to be occupied with thoughts about the architecture of his palace. He noticed that there was no water in the world of mermaids. Or had he adapted to their world so much that water had become invisible to him like the air is to humans?

Despite all the richness, colours, and beauty, there was something dreary about this place. Enjoyment itself was missing amidst all the objects of enjoyment floating around. He wondered whether it was because he hadn't earned those luxuries; rather, he had been tricked and forced onto them. His very existence as a merman was based on a trick, a deception, a lie. He gritted his teeth as his mind formed an image of the innocent green eyes of the mermaid who had tricked him into this spiritless existence.

Just as he was vowing never to forgive that mermaid, he heard a loud bang at the door.

'You are such a loser,' said the mermaid as she entered the room with her face flushed with anger, 'You couldn't lift me up the rock and came tumbling down instead. And you are calling me a liar and a cheater? Every word I spoke was truth. I know the place where boats pass by. I could have taken you there if only you had rescued me. Yes, I am a trapped soul waiting to be rescued. If you had converted me back to human form, we might have crossed the ocean and reached home by now.'

'What... what do you... is it possible to convert back to human form?' Urva rose from his bed and drew himself closer to the angry but innocuous face of the mermaid, his eyes dilated and gleaming with mingled hope and amazement.

The mermaid pulled away from him as though he were contaminated by a deadly disease. Picking up a crystal ball along the way, she reached the far end of the room and stood with her back against the wall.

'Don't you dare call me a liar and cheater,' she said warningly, pressing the crystal ball hard between her hands.

'I won't. I promise,' said Urva hastily, eyeing the crystal ball with suspicion. 'Please... is it possible to—'

'Yes, it is,' she shouted impatiently. 'It is a tug of war, you pathetic creature! If a man pulls a mermaid out of the water, she becomes a human. But if the man gets pulled into the water,' she scowled at him fiercely, 'he becomes a merman.'

'Can I go to the surface of the ocean and try my luck?' he asked hopefully, at the same time wondering why he had failed to pull such a slim creature up on the rock. The unspeakable beauty that intoxicated him then appeared quite ordinary now.

'No, you can't,' she frowned at him incredulously. 'Do you realize that you have just been transformed into a merman? You are an infant in this world. You will get your chance for freedom when you come of age. Only one chance. And I,' she threw the ball on the floor, frustrated, 'I—I have lost my chance, thank you very much.'

'Were you also a human before you got tricked into this world?' said Urva sympathetically.

'You haven't bothered to look beyond the beauty of this place, have you?' retorted the mermaid. 'Every single inhabitant in this kingdom was a human at some point in time. We don't reproduce. We convert humans into our kind. Each one of us is allowed only one descendent. You are my descendent because I have converted you. When you come of age, you will get your chance to hunt, which will be your chance for freedom too. You may either convert a human and grow your lineage here, or you may convert yourself back to human and reclaim your freedom.'

By the time Urva came of age, he had built such deep relationships with his fellow mer-people that he couldn't think of any freedom beyond the kingdom he lived in. He had all the pleasures he could possibly imagine except the pleasure of having a descendent to carry forward his legacy. This pleasure, too, was now hovering over him like a rain cloud. He couldn't wait for the day he would convert a human into a mer-human and enjoy the rest of his life mentoring his descendent.

The thought of death, however, was admittedly unsettling. He knew that just like his fellow mer-people, he would be fed alive to the whales one day in one of the sacrificial ceremonies that took place every fortnight. The elderly mer-people would enter the open mouths of the giant whales to pay for the protection provided to the kingdom by the whales. A horrifying death indeed. This was the only thought that unsettled him enough to desire to return to the human world where the possibility of having a peaceful death was quite high.

Finally, the day of hunting arrived. The tiny fishes that worked as slaves for mer-people had brought the information about the potential target. It was a sailor girl aboard a boat. She appeared to be lonely and broke.

Urva rose to the surface of the ocean and approached the side of the boat where the sailor girl sat hugging the deck railings with her legs wrapped around a baluster. Her gaze was resting upon the water, but her mind was far away. It took her a while to notice a fantastic, mesmerizing creature gliding along the boat right before her absent-minded gaze.

Urva had decided that he would not keep his victim in the dark about his identity and that he would speak the truth as directly as possible, unlike what his assailant had done to him many years ago. He made no efforts to hide his lower body. He made his first eye contact with the sailor girl only after having leapt several times out of the water and made full disclosure that he was a merman.

'Your friends are very loud, aren't they?' he said pointing to the loud voices and laughter issuing from inside the boat cabin.

As the girl's face contorted into a sorrowful expression, he hastily said, 'No… no… they are fine. No problem at all.'

He knew that attachment of any kind rising in the girl's heart towards him meant diminished chances of his freedom. She already seemed besotted by his handsome features, and the sorrowful feeling on top of that would be disastrous for his bid for freedom from the identity of a merman. Although it would make his alternate assignment, converting the girl into a mermaid, much easier for him.

Alternate assignment? Wasn't it the only assignment? To convert the sailor girl into a mermaid and enjoy the pleasures of having a descendent? Then why did he not let the girl sink beneath her sorrowful feeling and tumble off the boat? He resolved to trap the girl and make her his descendent so that his legacy could continue in the deep ocean.

'Feeling homesick?' he asked.

The girl didn't reply. A sudden moisture in her eyes indicated that something had melted in her heart. Chunks of loneliness, perhaps.

'I know this feeling. I have been away from home for years now,' said Urva, now gliding along so close to the boat that the girl had her head stuck out through the railing and inclined painfully to keep his charming face in view.

'Where—' she swallowed as her mouth was too dry. 'Where is your home?'

'It's across the ocean, but now I have forgotten how to reach there,' he said.

'I am also new to the ocean but my friends might help. Come on board.'

This was it. The sailor girl had expressed her desire, though indirectly, to help him. If she succeeded, he would become a human again. He shut his mind to all thoughts about the world of mermaids and mermen and leapt up at once.

Having hit the side of the boat and bounced back at first, he managed to get hold of the lower rail on the second attempt. His lower body started flopping violently, like a fish trying to get off the hook.

If there was a soul-crushing conflict between his upper body which was battling to hold onto the boat and his lower body which was struggling to get back into the water, it was nothing compared to the conflict that was escalating dramatically in his mind. The part of his mind that desired to regain human form worked hysterically to recycle his faded memories of his home across the ocean. The other part, the one that desired to stay a merman, inflated the feelings he had developed with his fellow mer-people: The feeling that he was indebted to the underwater kingdom for having enjoyed its pleasures for years, the feeling that he ought to have his own lineage in the deep ocean.

His upper body couldn't withstand the power of his lower body. Just as his hands lost contact with the rail, the sailor girl, who had been watching him stupefied until then, found her senses and managed to grab his arm.

She exerted all her strength to subdue the merman's violent body, but failed miserably. She toppled over and now she hung off the railing with just one hand somehow bearing weight of both of them.

Apart from a feeble, vanquished part of Urva that hoped that the girl gave up on him, his merman self was largely drawing pleasure at the ease with which his prey had fallen into his trap.

Attached as she was to the idea of helping Urva, she didn't let go of him, and eventually fell down into the water below. She had thereby, or so dictated the rulebook of the mer-people, expressed her desire to go wherever Urva went even if she had to transform into a mermaid. Once she fell into the water, Urva followed the rituals and converted her into a mermaid.

For many years to come, he enjoyed the pleasure of mentoring a descendent and the pride of having his own lineage in the deep ocean. Then came the day of his death. The ceremony of feeding him alive to a whale started. His upper, human body started jerking violently while his lower, fish body remained oblivious to the danger that loomed. He wanted to escape. Nobody was holding him in place, yet he couldn't move even an inch. He wanted to cry loudly but couldn't manage to let out even a bleat.

This utter helplessness eased suddenly as his upper body felt a jolt. He realized that it was just a nightmare. He was no merman. Nor was there any whale waiting to chew him alive. He was an ordinary man, Urva, who lay in the comfort and security of his hut. He breathed a deep sigh of relief and got up to drink water.

The memories of the nightmare were so fresh and haunting that he couldn't go back to sleep thereafter. He lay on his side with his legs curled up against his belly, hands tucked in between his knees, breath indiscernible, eyes open, and mind replaying the scenes of the nightmare he had woken from.

He had lost count of how many times he had seen this nightmare in the past, although this time it was much more clear and elaborate than before. Baba had promised him many years ago that he would stop seeing this nightmare once it reached a saturation point of clarity and detail. He hoped that this was the last time he endured this painful mental imagery. He couldn't wait to hear Baba's pronouncement on it.

'I was sitting on a rock in the middle of the ocean. I offered a hand to help a girl who stood in the water below. But she turned out to be a mermaid who converted me into a merman and led me into a dreary existence,' Urva told Baba when they were performing a daily ritual which involved trapping nine ants separately under nine coconut shells kept at the rim of the ceremony venue, giving oblations of cow butter into the fire, releasing one ant at a time and marking the path it took within a hand's distance from the rim, joining those markings to draw a zigzag line, and walking on that line at the end of the ceremony. This ritual signified the random and chaotic behaviour of a soul, in this particular case, the ant's soul, and imprints of its behaviour left on the world it sails through.

'And you are cursing that mermaid under your breath as usual, right?' asked Baba circling a scoop full of butter over a coconut shell which had an ant trapped underneath it. The rituals of the Mahtangs involved more talk on wisdom and less chanting of hymns.

'No Baba, that is what I wanted to tell you. Today I hold no grudges against that mermaid. I saw another part of the nightmare in which I was a merman out hunting an unsuspecting sailor girl. That made me understand the point of view of the mer-people. They don't hunt savagely. They convert a human into their kind only when the human expresses willingness, directly or indirectly, to go with them. While sitting on the rock, I had the choice to let go of the mermaid's hand, but I didn't. I can't hold the mermaid guilty of that,' said Urva.

Baba paused the ritual to look at Urva in amazement. This new development in the nightmare meant that Urva had come very close to becoming the Mahtang chieftain. It also meant that Lord Hanuman's arrival was very near. Or had He already arrived and started the process of the transfer of power, and of course responsibilities, from Baba to his descendent, Urva? Baba felt a wave of euphoria travelling through his body.

Baba had been containing his joy with the assumption that the figure he had seen last evening on the Ancestors' Cliff was not the real Lord Hanuman but a delusion played in his mind. As this assumption shattered in his mind, words trickled through his mouth, 'Lord Hanuman has arrived.'

These words, somehow, didn't reach Urva, nor did he notice any movement on Baba's lips.

Baba wondered why Lord Hanuman didn't want His arrival announced and celebrated. He didn't delve deeper into this, and instead settled on the convenient conclusion that his mind was too small to understand the ways of his immortal Guru.

'This is a very significant development, Urva. The mystery of this nightmare shall stand unravelled before you sooner than you can imagine,' said Baba, and then he returned to the rituals.

'Does that mean I will soon know what this mermaid mystery is all about?'

'Yes, indeed. You deserve to know this, at the very

least. I shall tell you about the mermaid whenever I see it today. It often wanders around us, very easy to spot,' said Baba, walking back towards the fire to make an oblation of the butter he had just enchanted over a coconut shell.

An hour later, after having breakfast, Urva, his best friend Dhanushka, their uncle Basantha, and Baba set out to hunt for honey. Just as they crossed the edge of their hamlet, Baba spotted three oddly-garbed outsider men, who seemed to have tried their best to look like jungle dwellers, sitting on three separate stones.

'There they are, three mermaids out to hunt me,' said Baba, flushed with anger, dropping his gaze from the three men and looking resolutely at the ground.

'I see no mermaid there, Baba. They are three men, perhaps wanting to talk to you,' said Urva, having shot a shifty glance at the three outsiders. Urva had always been curious about the people that lived outside the jungle, but not so much that he would go exploring their territory at the cost of facing the fury and wrath of Baba who considered them greedy monsters out to swallow the jungle.

'Oh yes, you are right and I'm wrong,' Baba shouted at Urva aggressively.

Urva didn't look discomfited, for he knew Baba was not angry at him but pretending to be so, thinking that the feigned anger would drive away the outsiders or at least kill their desire to talk to him.

But these outsiders were no ordinary tourists. One of the three, who called himself Hanudas, meaning the one surrendered to Lord Hanuman, had glimpsed the immortal Hanuman in broad daylight, amidst the noise of crowded streets in the city of Toronto. His two companions, Swamiji and Brahmachariji, who would adopt the title of *Hanudas* later, were highly knowledgeable monks. All three of them would later get assimilated by the Mahtangs and become the messengers who carried the words of the immortal Hanuman to mainstream society.

Much to the displeasure of Baba, his angry demeanour didn't deter the three intruders from walking up to him and saying something in an alien language. Whatever they said, they did it very politely and respectfully with their heads slightly bowed and hands joined in front of their chests.

Baba reacted as though it was Urva who had brought about this intrusion: He snatched the empty honey pot from his hands, slammed it on the ground right at his feet, shouted at him for no particular reason while the loud bang of the shattered pot added to the dramatic effect. The three intruders backed away with their hands raised slightly, trying to express categorically that their intentions were not to harm the tribal people or the jungle in any way.

When the path was clear, Baba, Urva, and other two Mahtangs marched off on their way to hunt honey.

'Wow, that was very fine acting,' giggled Urva once they were out of sight of the outsiders.

Baba frowned at him. His uncle Basantha started humming to himself, endeavouring to unhear what he believed was a mindless utterance from the mouth of the future leader of Mahtangs.

Urva had been pronounced as the next leader when he was nine years old. Since then, he had been subjected to suffocating expectations from his community members. Everyone expected him to comport himself with the maturity of an 80-year-old. They would search every word he spoke for the message of the gods. He had learned to withhold his youthful impulses. He had a filter in place inside his mind which reduced every urge to guffaw into a smile, every impulse of mindless chatter into silence. Only his friend Dhanushka understood him for what he really was, a typical young man. Urva had never been able to fully understand why the gods had chosen him to be the next head of the Mahtangs.

'Good that we now have one less honey pot to fill,' said Dhanushka with the haste of a man trying to mask the wrongdoing of his best friend.

'Baba, who is the mermaid? Did you see it in those three men?' asked Urva, back to doing what was expected of him: talking wisdom.

'Any soul you are attached to is a mermaid for you because it slowly pulls you into the pond of its bad Karma,' replied Baba, returning to his pleasant self.

'Baba, I am attached to my best friend Dhanushka. Is his soul transferring its bad Karma to me?' asked Urva as he earnestly tried to understand the allegory of the mermaid.

'Yes, if you are attached to him you are being slowly dragged by his soul, the mermaid, into the dark pool of all the bad Karma it may have,' replied Baba, turning his head to spare a suspicious glance at Dhanushka who was walking behind them.

'Attachment is bad, yeah,' commented Dhanushka, who seemed eager to convey that he hadn't taken Baba's words personally and that he was equally interested in knowing the mystery of the nightmares his friend had been enduring since childhood.

'Come on Dhanu, it doesn't make any sense. If there is a transfer of bad Karma taking place between us because of the attachment, it has to be mutual. If we imagine attachment as a channel between two souls, the flow can't be one-sided,' said Urva airily.

'If the attachment is mutual, then transfer is mutual. The souls of both of you are mermaids for each other in that scenario,' said Baba politely.

'And if attachment establishes a channel between two souls, bad and good Karma should equally flow through it. It can't be the transfer of only bad Karma,' said Urva. It appeared he wasn't listening to Baba.

'You know what? Forget about it. You aren't ready yet to know the mystery of the mermaid,' said Baba, frowning heavily.

'Yes, Baba, I agree. I shall be ready, I guess, when my nightmares have tortured me into lunacy,' said Urva, snipping off a cluster of leaves in frustration as he passed under a low branch of a gnarled tree.

Long minutes passed. The four Mahtangs added no sound of their own to the ambience of the jungle except for the sound of heavy breathing from Baba as they trudged on the rough terrain.

A sudden thought erupted in Urva's mind. The thought was too scholastically exciting to bother about its source. He expressed it immediately, 'Baba, suppose there is a famous musician. People from all over the kingdom are his fans. This is a one-sided attachment. That means his soul is a mermaid transferring its bad Karma to thousands of his fans. As a result, he lives a life of abundance while his fans struggle with difficulties of day-to-day life. His bad Karma affect his fans.'

'You can understand anything when you want to,' complemented Baba without softening his tone. 'You got it absolutely right, Urva. If you are attached to a soul, it behaves like a mermaid and transfers its bad Karma to you. You can imagine the mermaid as someone who is suffering from an infectious disease. They infect anyone who gets attached to them. They may not do it intentionally. It just happens because that is the nature of a soul; it wants to get rid of bad Karma and possess good Karma. Therefore, by the sheer nature of a soul, only the bad Karma flow through the channel of attachment unless some artificial means are deployed to alter the natural process. Your friend Dhanushka's soul, assuming you are attached to him, is a mermaid infecting you with its bad Karma. It doesn't mean that he is intentionally doing it. One mustn't hold grudges against the mermaid. Just take care not to get attached to it. Patients with an infectious disease don't intend to infect you. It just happens if you come in contact with them.'

'How come the souls of those outsiders act as mermaids on you, Baba? You are not friends with them, are you? I don't see any attachment between you and them. What am I missing?' asked Dhanushka, his voice beginning to crack; the head of the tribe had accused him of 'infecting' his successor.

'Being angry at someone is also a form of attachment, Dhanu,' replied Urva before Baba could prepare his answer.

'Yes, thank you, Urva,' said Baba. 'Every emotion is a form of attachment. There are mainly nine emotions: Joy, Sadness, Anger, Fear, Pity, Disgust, Expectation, Surprise, and Trust. You are attached to those who give you joy. You are attached to those who make you sad. You are attached to those you fear. You are attached to those you are full of pity for. You are attached to those who disgust you. You are attached to those you expect from. You are attached to those who surprise you. You are attached to those you trust. In short, you are attached to those who evoke any kind of emotion in you. You should consider them all as mermaids, or the infected souls out to sink you in the depths of their bad Karma.'

'In that case, every living soul we come across is a potential mermaid,' remarked Dhanushka with a sense of relief in his voice.

'The stronger the attachment, though, the quicker and higher the transmission of bad Karma,' said Baba. He hadn't directed his remark at Urva and Dhanushka's friendship but Dhanushka saw it hitting just there. Urva, meanwhile, was busy in his own calculations.

'A king is loved by some and hated by others but, since hate and love both fall under the definition of attachment, he is attached to all. His soul, therefore, transfers its bad Karma to all. Funny, isn't it? The mathematics of Karma rains luxuries on him at the expense of both his fans and haters,' uttered Urva, preoccupied with his own thoughts.

Dhanushka didn't let the conversation pivot in another direction. Resolute on finding out what Baba actually thought of his friendship with Urva, he said, 'Indeed, we have a strong attachment. We must be flooding each other with our bad Karma.'

'Maybe the flow of bad Karma has reached an equilibrium between you two,' said uncle Basantha, joining the conversation for the first time.

'Yes, that is likely,' said Baba. 'Many factors come into play when two souls attach to each other. We are currently discussing the broad allegory of the mermaid.'

'I am being brutalized by the nightmares just to understand this?' asked Urva. 'Even a child could master this allegory in a minute. Why the torture, Baba? I spend years in one night trapped in the kingdom of mer-people and then I am fed alive to giant whales. I can't describe the agony.'

'Once you take charge as the chieftain, you must be able to spot the mermaid immediately and save yourself and your subjects from it. It sounds easy but it's very tricky. We tend to underestimate the deadly power of the mermaid because it usually hides inside mortal, ordinary people. To be honest, even I am feeling very weak today. I think the mermaids that skulked behind those outsiders have infected me to some extent,' said Baba.

As he spoke these words, the mental images of the three 'greedy intruders' flashed in his mind, causing a ripple of anger that he contained immediately. This lingering residue of anger suggested weakness in his defences against the mermaid. He could feel an air of ordinariness around him ever since he had returned from the Ancestors' Cliff last evening with the news that Lord Hanuman had arrived. He had been feeling like a relieved trustee who was about to hand the property back over to its owner. This little weakness could have alarmed him on an ordinary day, but not today, for he knew Lord Hanuman was there to rescue him in case the mermaid sank him.

'It was your anger that became the channel between

the mermaid and you. What real harm could it do to you, Baba? A spoiled mood for a day or two, a little headache maybe? What else?' asked Urva.

'Here you go, your question proves my point,' said Baba. 'You haven't understood the mermaid yet. You are talking about the side-effects of anger while I am talking about the harm done by transmitted bad Karma. The impact of the latter is very real and mostly immediate. I can't tell how much and what kind of their bad Karma got transmitted into my soul through the channel of anger. It can wreak havoc in my life immediately or some day later. Memory of this incident and the anger it sparks may fade away in a few days but the bad Karma won't vanish without causing the trouble they are meant to cause. Worse still, my soul may transfer them, unintentionally of course, to my fellow Mahtangs, the same people I am supposed to protect.'

'An example could help, Baba,' said Basantha, while Urva drove the horses of imagination to catch Baba's words in their true essence.

'I don't mean to create fear here since fear is also a form of attachment, but if you want examples of the harm that the transmitted bad Karma could cause, imagine me or my loved ones meeting a nasty accident,' said Baba.

'Meeting a nasty accident just because you got angry at a bunch of aliens?' asked Dhanushka.

'I repeat, anger only lays the channel, the flow of bad Karma causes the harm,' said Baba.

'And there is no escape from this harm, is there?' asked Basantha. Even though he was much older than his nephews, in terms of knowledge he stood at equal footing with them. He was a young child, ineligible to get the supreme knowledge, when the immortal Guru had visited the Mahtangs 41 years ago.

'We can certainly choose not to build contacts outside our community,' said Dhanushka. 'That way, we exchange Karma only with each other. Being Mahtangs, we don't hold much bad Karma with us anyway.'

'Or…' started Baba, expecting Urva to complete his sentence.

Urva didn't disappoint. He said, 'Or we can feign emotions instead of actually being emotional, just the way you did, Baba. You weren't actually angry at them. You were only acting. Fine acting, though.'

'And the same goes for our interactions within our community too,' said Baba. 'The wise Mahtangs stay away from all nine forms of attachment, all the emotions. We express emotions as though we are acting in a play: the grand play of Maya.'

'True emotions make a true human being. Only the selfish people fake their emotions to weave their evil designs,' said Dhanushka, looking enquiringly at Urva.

'Faking and acting are different, Dhanu,' said Urva. 'I can have true emotions at any given time and be simultaneously aware that this world is just a grand play wherein I am merely playing a character.'

'This awareness comes with knowledge, the supreme knowledge which Lord Hanuman had imparted to me and other senior Mahtangs 41 years ago,' said Baba.

'You two,' said Basantha nodding towards his nephews, 'weren't even born then and I was just a child, ineligible to absorb even a single word from our immortal Guru,' he said with a gleam of longing in his eyes. He, like Urva and Dhanuska, was unaware that their immortal Guru had arrived again after 41 years.

'Those who have realized the supreme truth, the Brahmanas, too experience joy,' said Baba, 'but they do it as though they are playing a joyful character; they too get sad, but as though they are playing a sad character; they too get angry, but as though they—'

'I got it, Baba,' Urva cut across him. 'If we express our emotions with the awareness of being a character in this grand play, we remain safe from the mermaid.'

'There it is, one more mermaid,' said Baba a minute later when they had detoured off their honey-hunting trail in pursuit of the source of a putrid smell and found an almost dead, maggot-infested dog dumped beside a bush. Though the strong, nauseating smell didn't allow them to crouch near the dog and inspect, Baba's steady gaze spotted a sign of life in what otherwise looked like a mass of dead flesh and bones with flies swarming all over the filthy, stinking wounds.

'Basantha, you go and bring the poisonous herbs for killing maggots. You know where to find them; yes, the lakeside. Take Dhanushka with you for help. Go and come back quickly,' instructed Baba, suddenly brusque.

When Basantha and Dhanushka had dashed off, Baba turned around to give instructions to Urva, 'and Urva, you—'

But Urva was nowhere to be seen.

'Urva!' Baba called out loudly.

'No… you can't do this to me,' bleated Urva from

behind a tree about thirty steps away from where Baba stood.

The expression on Baba's face was that of a parent dealing with their child who had just invented a new tantrum. He strode over to Urva and frogmarched him back near the dog.

'Since when have you become so squeamish that you can't stand even the sight of a badly wounded animal?' barked Baba.

'Mermaid,' mumbled Urva, his gaze transfixed on the spot where the dog lay, his face white like that of a prisoner facing the gallows.

Baba's eyes sparkled. With a small grin and suppressed excitement, he said, 'Mermaid, yes! Great that you see it. Yes, this dog evokes strong emotion of pity in us. Pity is also a form of attachment. Therefore, its soul should be regarded as a mermaid which can potentially sink us into its bad Karma. But we can't stop being who we are merely because there is a risk of soul contamination involved here. Running away without exerting all our efforts to help the dog is like stabbing our soul from fear of contamination, or like committing suicide on the rock from fear of drowning in the sea below. Therefore, we won't stop being sympathetic. We won't run away from the emotion of pity and the action it triggers. We will help the dog but as though we are playing a character of someone who is sympathetic and helpful—are you with me, Urva?'

Urva wasn't listening. He had seen the mermaid for the first time in the waking state. He was looking at it with his eyes slightly twitching and mouth agape. Baba, with the happiness of a person who was about to become a grandparent, relieved Urva from the esoteric speech and instructed him to go back to the honey hunting trail.

After watching Urva slouch away and out of sight, Baba had nobody to talk to. He crouched near the dog to examine its wounds, holding his breath against the strong, foul smell.

His eyes had fallen on the dog's terribly wounded head only for a moment. The hideous image his mind captured in that moment wouldn't fade even a little until his dying day: Slimy, writhing, disgusting maggots eating their way into eye sockets, half the head already devoured.

With a great shudder, Baba leapt to his feet, staggered back several steps and gulped a lungful of air. Disgusted, repulsed and incensed, his mind went into overdrive picturing how he would spill the poison over the maggots and kill them all at once. After replaying this image a number of times, his anger shifted to Basantha and Dhanushka who had gone to fetch the poisonous herbs.

'What is holding up those deplorable two?' he cursed through gritted teeth even though they were well within time. They were collecting the required herbs at the lakeside about a mile away from there. It was Baba whose minutes were now passing like long hours. He had sunk beneath the intense emotions sparked by the terrible sight of the dog's head teeming with maggots.

A few minutes later, however, having been bitten by a poisonous snake, both Basantha and Dhanuska's unconscious bodies lay in the thickets at the lakeside, foam dribbling out of their mouths. The supposed delay in their return was now a hard reality. It was no longer an imagination of Baba's restive mind.

For someone familiar with the allegory of the mermaid, it was no random accident. The maggots collectively had a soul which acted like a mermaid on Baba. It transmitted its bad Karma through the channel created by his emotion of disgust. The poison that he imagined would kill the maggots was now flowing in the veins of his loved ones.

He had spotted the mermaid inside the dog, but he had failed to see the mermaid that existed in the writhing cluster of maggots. He couldn't kill the maggots and liberate them from their dreary existence. Rather, the maggots had pulled him into a possible dreary existence where he would live with the reality of losing two of his loved ones.

Baba left the spot with the resolve that he would come back speedily to heal the dog, and ran towards the lake where he had sent Basantha and Dhanushka to fetch the herbs. When he reached the bank of the lake, he didn't know which way to turn to look for his loved ones; the poisonous herbs they were supposed to collect were available on both sides of the lake. He shouted their names maniacally. Then he paused to hear the response. No human voice reached his ears; his agitated mind registered the frantic, ominous chirping of a flock of birds. They were hopping from branch to branch in a tree that stood tall and straight amidst a thicket of small bushes several meters away to his right.

Even as his feet launched him in the direction of the chirping birds, his mind had drawn the rough sketch of the scene his eyes were about to meet. What he saw seconds later was worse than his worst nightmares.

Limp and possibly lifeless bodies... Alarmingly pale blue skin... Red blazing snakebite wounds... Eyes open and rolled in the bulging sockets... Crusts of white saliva drying down the corners of open mouths...

With trembling hands, Baba untied the sacred black thread that he wore around his waist, hastily broke it into two, and sank to his shaking knees beside Basantha's motionless body. He tied the piece of thread around the swollen calf, scarified the wound with his knife, and began sucking and spitting the poisoned blood.

Basantha's body remained as unmoved and lifeless as before. Horrified and devastated, Baba scrambled over to Dhanushka's body and repeated the same process of sucking and spitting the blood.

Not even a single flicker of life showed. The venom had spread to their brains. It was too late for any treatment to work. Baba shook the nearly dead bodies violently, shouting names of both of his loved ones as though trying to wake them up from a deep sleep. His cracking voice eventually died. As he stared at the pale blue face of Dhanushka, his eyes filled with tears and his vision became blurred.

Blurred vision felt to him as though death was pulling dark curtains over the last window of hope. A fresh alarm of horror rang in his mind. He staggered to his feet and shouted Urva's name, thinking that he might be in the vicinity.

He didn't know what difference Urva's or anybody else's presence could make when he, the wisest of the Mahtangs, was all out of options. He perhaps wanted Death to know that he had not conceded defeat yet and that she couldn't take away his loved ones while he was still exploring options.

When he didn't receive any response from Urva, his weakened mind started manufacturing images in which Urva's body too lay lifeless not too far away. Another part of his mind countered these images by cursing Urva for turning a deaf ear to his screams.

The anger suddenly found its way to a screeching monkey that was jumping on the branches of a tree nearby. This monkey had a bunch of anti-poison leaves in one hand and a banana in the other.

It reminded him that no Mahtang had ever died of a snakebite before, thanks to the close association of his community with the monkeys that were trained to bring the fresh leaves of anti-poison herbs whenever a Mahtang asked for them.

Basantha and Dhanushka must have raised the screech of help before they collapsed. That explained why the monkey had the bunch of anti-poison leaves in its hand. But nothing could explain why it hadn't thrown the leaves near the needy, and why it was happily munching a banana when it ought to be screeching to gather other monkeys for help.

Baba went mental: He grabbed a stone and threw it at the monkey who ducked and mimicked him by throwing the banana peels at him. When the unkind creature jumped from the tree and ran, Baba chased it with a stick in hand.

From a person so wise that he had the authority to speak to the gods, to a person belligerently chasing a monkey for no reason, Baba had sunk to immeasurable depths of ignorance and evil in less than an hour.

Not one, but three mermaids had buried him in this darkness: First, the mermaid inside the maggots to which he got attached through the emotion of disgust; second, the mermaids inside the lifeless figures of his loved ones to which he got attached through the emotion of fear; third, the mermaid inside the monkey to which he got attached through the emotion of anger.

He dragged his tired, old body behind the monkey until an unendurable pain rose in his chest. He bent low, his hands on his knees, and gasped violently for air, sweat streaming off every inch of his body. The monkey, who seemed to have enjoyed the chase, perched happily on a low branch of the nearest tree.

Under the same tree, Urva sat peacefully, facing the tree trunk, his lips moving as though talking to it. Even though Baba stood panting and grunting loudly only a few steps away from him, both remained oblivious to each other's presence for several minutes.

Eventually, Baba's breath normalized. He lifted his head and saw Urva's back.

'Urva—you—' Baba yelled, wheezing. 'You useless lump of flesh, what are you doing sitting here? I have been shouting my lungs out for you—'

Urva, who had flashed a look of utter shock and bewilderment over his shoulder, was now looking at the tree trunk as before.

Baba's mind nearly exploded with renewed rage, directed this time towards what he thought was the disobedient and careless behaviour of Urva. He lunged forward, apparently to teach Urva a lesson, but back to back stabs of severe chest pain paralyzed him. Clutching the left side of his chest with both hands, giving a cry of pain which got stuck in his throat, he first stooped low, then dropped to his knees and lay upon the ground. The pain went away, but so did his consciousness.

Urva glanced once again over his shoulder and saw Baba collapsed on the ground. He remained seated in his place as though what was happening right behind his back was not real. The only figure that was real for him stood in front of him, leaning comfortably against the tree trunk: the immortal Lord Hanuman.

'… And then he chased the monkey and reached here. He saw you, but not me. He thought you were talking to the tree,' said Lord Hanuman, explaining why Baba behaved strangely.

'But… But why, Deva? Why couldn't he see you?' asked Urva.

'The same reason why millions of other souls on this planet can't see me: Bad Karma, the deep pit of bad Karma that exists between me and them. Baba got buried under a multi-layered veil of ignorance in just one hour by… by the mermaids, if I may put it allegorically,' replied Lord Hanuman.

'Deva, if getting disgusted by a swarm of maggots, getting fearful at the sight of loved ones in danger, and getting angry at an unfaithful monkey is the reason why Baba is buried under bad Karma, then I should be too, for I have been intensely disgusted, horrified, and angered many times in the past,' said Urva.

'Yes, you and many of your fellow Mahtangs have sunk to the depths of bad Karma by the mermaid several times in the past. But you and your community members were subsequently rescued from the clutches of the mermaid—.'

'How, Deva? You were away from us for the last 41 years. Then who rescued the Mahtangs who kept getting lured by the mermaid from time to time?' asked Urva.

'Baba rescued them,' replied Lord Hanuman simply. 'Yes, Baba has been guarding the Mahtang community against the mermaid. And for the next 41 years, once I depart from here, it shall be your responsibility as the Mahtang chieftain to rescue anyone in your community who stepped into the trap of the mermaid.'

'But, Deva, I am not prepared for such a huge responsibility,' said Urva at once. 'Who will rescue me if I myself get trapped?'

'You won't get trapped. You can't afford to. The painful and sleepless nights full of tormenting dreams you have been enduring since childhood, coupled with the knowledge that I shall impart to you while I am here, will help you spot the mermaid immediately,' said Lord Hanuman.

'But... but Baba himself got trapped today, didn't he?' Urva turned his head and saw Baba still collapsed on the ground behind him.

'Baba didn't falter even once in the last 41 years. His guard against the mermaids is weak only since last evening when he saw that I am here to take care of the Mahtangs. And that is quite understandable—the fatigue of 41 years, you see. In any case, it is a great opportunity for you to learn how to free someone from the slavery of the mermaids. Tell me... what would you do if I weren't here talking to you?' asked Lord Hanuman.

'Baba's unusual behaviour and the news of Basantha and Dhanuska's accident would have evoked strong fear in me. Fear means attachment, attachment to the mermaid. I would have spotted the mermaid inside Baba and acted as though I am in the grand play of Maya. With that awareness, I would have accompanied Baba to—'

'That way,' interrupted his immortal Guru, 'you would have saved your soul from further contamination from the mermaid, but what about Baba's soul which has already been contaminated? How do we reverse that? Because of the bad Karma he got from the maggots, two of his loved ones had an accident. How do we reverse that? Even if you went with him and revived the victims, the memory of the accident would still be there. The mermaid's effect will stay in the form of the memory. You know very well that a memory planted in your mind has the power to alter your future actions. Memories of the past one hour would influence the future of Mahtangs for years to come. To free Baba and your entire community from the effect of the mermaid, you need to undo everything it has caused, undo it in such a way that even the slightest trace of memory isn't left.'

'But how, Deva?' asked Urva.

Lord Hanuman's reply came in the form of what was a miracle in Urva's view: Baba woke up behind Urva, yawning, as though from a nice nap and called out Dhanuska's name, asking whether he was done collecting the honey. Dhanushka, who was perched at the top of a nearby tree under which stood Basantha, replied that it was almost done.

Yes, the two members of the Mahtang community who lay unconscious with poison running in their veins a short while ago were not only healthy but also free from memories of the troubles they had gone through. However, for some reason, Urva's memories remained unchanged.

'H... how, Deva?' asked Urva, bewildered.

'You will learn it from me in the coming days while I am stationed here,' replied his immortal Guru.

The conversation between the Guru and the disciple broke as Baba, who had seen Lord Hanuman, joined in, followed by Basantha and Dhanushka.

Chapter 3
Describing the Indescribable

Even as Baba, Urva, Dhanushka, and Basantha inhaled the stinking smell that led them to the dying, maggot-infested dog and all the attendant events, a group of six Mahtang women inhaled a horrifying smell on their way to collecting firewood. It alerted them of the presence of a leopard nearby. They retreated immediately and decided to take another path to reach their destination. This meant that they had to return all the way to their hamlet and trudge on a long, winding path to reach the spot where they had trimmed a number of trees for firewood the previous day.

'Pathetic! We are pathetic puppets. We are not even able to walk on the path we desire to walk. The idea of freewill is false, I tell you. The unknown, invisible powers are driving us the way they want,' snapped Basantha's wife Janakirupa, a short, plump, middle-aged Mahtang woman, once they were a safe distance away from the horrifying smell of the leopard.

'A myth in one kingdom might be a truth in another,' said Urmi, an average height, thin Mahtang woman in her early twenties. 'I have seen Baba perform impossible tasks with his freewill. The elders of our community don't show their powers but they do exercise their freewill to the fullest extent whenever the need arises. The knowledge makes all the difference, I suppose. They received the supreme knowledge from Lord Hanuman 41 years ago when we weren't even born. Our souls were walking the Earth through some other bodies.'

'My soul was right here. I had been born, you hadn't,' Janakirupa corrected her. 'But of course, I was an infant, hadn't learned so much as a word.'

Urmi and Janakirupa, despite an age difference of about 20 years between them, were best friends. For the inquisitive mind of Urmi, every inch of the jungle was a page of the absolute book of wisdom. She would stare at the flora and fauna for hours as though reading an engrossing book. Her highly scholarly attitude coupled with her mania for protecting every fabric of the Mahtang culture never allowed her to mingle with women of her age. As she was often described by her community members, she was an 80-year-old mind trapped into a 20-year-old body. Every Mahtang, young or old, male or female, respected her especially because the gods had declared her to be the future wife of the next Mahtang chieftain, Urva.

'Let's cease to be puppets right from this moment. ... Let's walk the path we desire to walk. ... Let's return to the path that is swept by the smell of the leopard. ...' said Janakirupa, smirking slightly, and observing reaction on Urmi's face.

'No, that would be against the rules. We Mahtangs, as you are very much aware, never take the path where a leopard has left its smell,' came the reply from Urmi, just as Janakirupa had expected. Had this proposal been put before Urva, he would have plunged into making it a reality. But Urmi was different; different from Urva, different from all Mahtangs of her age group. She believed in following and, if possible, in enforcing rules and customs. And her brilliant mind never failed her in supplying the necessary rationale for doing so.

After a thoughtful pause, Urmi found the rationale for not breaking the rule as she added, 'In any case, we wouldn't stop being puppets even if we ignored our fears and walked on the path laden with the danger of the leopard. I mean, there are millions of paths on the Earth where humans are walking right now as we speak. For days to come, we will not walk one of those paths because we will have the information of a leopard associated with it. But what about the rest of the paths? We will never walk most of them in our entire lifetime. Why? Puppets, we are! The mighty puppeteer has thrown us into this part of the world to crawl a bunch of paths of this jungle all our lives.'

'Puppeteer? There could be not one but several puppeteers—the higher powers that limit our freewill,' said Janakirupa, distractedly. The new path they were trekking offered plenty of food for her curious mind.

'Maybe there are none,' said Urmi, taking in the surroundings as curiously as her best friend. 'I sometimes feel that we are lost inside an enormous maze. It is quite possible that no one is purposefully controlling us. Maybe we are trapped inside a maze, and we are hitting dead-ends because we have no clue which path is the correct one. Maybe the purpose of our life is to find the path that would take us out of this—watch out!'

She had spotted a sharp thorn in Janakirupa's way but by the time she raised alarm, her friend had already crossed over it safely.

'Watch out for what?' asked Janakirupa having stopped dead in her tracks.

'Never mind,' said Urmi. She took a step backward as other women of the group watched her with an amused expression on their faces, bent low and picked up a long, sharp thorn from the ground.

Showing it to Janakirupa, she said, 'It was in your path. You didn't see it. An invisible power saved you from it. Or was it just luck?'

'Perhaps what you said is right,' said Janakirupa, holding out a hand to take the thorn from Urmi. 'We are inside a maze, encountering circumstances at random. If we knew the paths in the maze, we would walk them at our will. In ignorance, we are just rolling on without any direction.'

'Partial ignorance, I would say,' said Urmi, looking towards a berry tree. 'For instance, I know exactly how to get berries from that tree, but I don't know how to become a queen.'

'Full ignorance, I would think,' said Janakirupa. 'You know that you can walk to that tree, throw a stone into it and get the berries. But you don't know that you might encounter something on the way that could stop you from reaching the tree. Furthermore, why is there any need to walk to that tree and do anything of that sort? Why can't you desire to get the berries at this moment and get them in the next moment?'

Urmi didn't seem convinced about the 'full ignorance' argument even though she had no argument to offer to the contrary, not at that moment anyway. She and Janakirupa remained silent for the rest of their journey, much to the respite of the other four women in the group.

'Demon attack,' shouted Urmi when she was collecting firewood about half an hour later and felt her arms twitch involuntarily. Initially, she thought she was imagining it. When her entire body jerked, she shouted with all her might to alert her group which had dispersed to work individually. Janakirupa and other four women converged on her and assessed the scene. They steered her to a safe place and removed nearby sharp objects that might injure her as she struggled with 'the demon' that had overpowered her body.

It was a seizure attack, and it was not the first time she was battling this demon. This horrible experience had been a regular affair in her life since childhood. It was a storm that would come into her body unbidden and leave scars mostly on her psyche and sometimes on her body.

Her hands flailed violently, her feet kicked erratically, her face contorted horribly, her body writhed in soul-tearing agony, and her tongue let out incomprehensible words in some alien language as her friends watched her piteously and helplessly.

Unnoticed by any of them were two strangers watching her stealthily and curiously from behind a distant tree. These two men were neither Mahtangs nor from any other tribal community. They were two of the three outsiders who had been rebuked by Baba a short while ago.

When the seizure subsided, she carefully lay down upon the ground under the shade of a tree. Her friends left her there and resumed their work. Her body was aggrieved, exhausted, and tired but her mind attempted to release some thoughts, some questions, some grievances.

What had demons found so delicious in her flesh and blood that they wanted to feast on it? What did she lack that the gods had found her unworthy of protecting from demons? She hadn't as much as hurt an ant in her living memory. Then why was she being subjected to pain time and again?

She had the answers to each of her questions. But at that moment the questions seemed more alleviating than the answers. Tears rolled down out of the corners of her eyes. She didn't try to blink them back. Nor did she try to extricate answers from the depths of her intellect, the answers that might have explained her pain and stopped the tears.

Her grievance that the gods were not protecting her was unfounded. In fact, the twin gods of health, the Ashwins, were present at her side and doing everything they could do. They had arrived to help her even before the first sign of the seizure emerged. They had tried to contain the seizure but failed like they had every time the seizures had struck her in the past.

The therapy used by the Ashwin twins to cure a disease is unique in its own way. It is based on the fact that every diseased body has its corresponding healthy body present in the alternative plane of existence. The soul can switch from the diseased body to the healthy body in no time, but the illusionary external world, Maya, keeps the soul trapped in the diseased body. It keeps the soul believing that the diseased body is the only reality. It uses many ways to do so.

If the soul could be freed from the claws of Maya even for an instant, it could make the desired switch. That is precisely what the Ashwin twins try to do. For them, curing a disease is like a war with Maya. If they win, the disease is cured. Else, as it happened in Urmi's case, the disease persists.

The Ashwins were invisible to every living soul present at the scene. Urmi, who lay there with her eyes closed, was also unaware of their presence. Lord Hanuman arrived there a short while later. Being a Mahtang, Urmi was supposed to sense at least His presence. Perhaps the storm of thoughts raging in her mind acted as an opaque veil between her and her immortal Guru. Although one of the strangers huddled behind a distant tree did notice three quivering, faint figures.

'Hanuman, we know that Mahtangs are very dear to you; you can't see them in pain. But in the case of Urmi, we are helpless. We have applied all our knowledge and expertise, but so far we have failed to identify the weapon being used by Maya to keep her soul inside the diseased body,' said the Ashwins regretfully as they stood on either side of Urmi, their heads bowed a little and hands clasped in front of them.

Lord Hanuman moved from beside Urmi's feet towards her head, His eyes fixed on her pale face ablaze with direct sunlight falling through the tree leaves. He sat down on a stone beside Urmi's head. (This stone was not there a moment ago.) The Ashwins followed; they sat down on either side of Urmi.

Lord Hanuman spoke as though crooning to a child. His words, however, were heard only by the Ashwins as he said, 'Dear Ashwins, I know what Maya is using to keep her soul in illusion. I have a plan to shatter this illusion to bits. Let's execute it.'

Lord Hanuman's healing plan included reminding Urmi of an important sequence from her previous life. Injecting information of forgotten past and unseen future has immediate and far reaching consequences on the journey of the soul. Therefore, the seers administrating this injection should know what they are doing, and they should first prepare the soul for the injection by giving it sufficient knowledge of Karma, Desire, Time, Space, Maya and everything else that might be necessary for the case at hand.

Lord Hanuman closed His eyes. The Ashwin twins joined their hands in the air to make a lotus shape right above the Muladhara Chakra (Root Chakra) of Urmi's body. Lord Hanuman's lips started moving but His words didn't travel even an inch through the air; they echoed directly in Urmi's mind, describing the indescribable:

Urmi, my child, you are tired. Let me regale you with the wonders of this universe as you submit yourself to a healing sleep.

To you, this universe looks like an endless expanse comprising stars, planets, and other celestial bodies. Have you ever wondered what it looks like to someone who is not bound by Time and Space?

I can be free from the grip of Space-Time at my will. Once I go out of the boundaries of Time, everything that has happened, is happening, and will happen doesn't remain a mystery. Words and phrases like past, present, future, happened, happening, and will-happen make no sense to me. It looks like everything has already taken place. I can see all the occurrences of the Universe collectively, at once.

Just imagine what it would look like if all the scenes

that have taken place over the course of millions of years are put together.

This universe looks like a quiet, shining white ball of strange fluid when perceived from outside Space-Time. This fluid is held together in spherical form by a web of thin strings spread all through it. This white fluid is the fluid of Space. These strings are that of Time, also known as T-strings.

To you, as a human being who is trapped in Space-Time, this universe seems to be made up of objects. You classify them as small, big, living, non-living, and so on. For someone like me who is free from Space-Time, the Universe consists of scenes. I can choose any scene and live it as though it's happening with me.

For a minute, just drop your identity, 'Urmi', and assume that you have escaped from both Time and Space. You have no identity, no mind, no memories; you are nothing because if you were something, you would be in the Space-Time, not outside it. If the *nothingness* is hard to imagine, imagine that you are just a speck of light.

I see that you are still lingering in the identity of Urmi. Drop it. You are *nothing*, you are Shunya.

You, a speck of light, are ready to go inside the ball of Space-Time to live a scene out of the infinite number of scenes happening there. (Or have already happened, whatever you would like to call it.)

Let's say you want to live the following scene: A young man called Vaibhav is eating delicious mangoes in a forest as a carpet of red flowers decorates the landscape, the sweet sound of chirping birds creates a soothing ambience, and the smell of ripe fruits and scented flowers permeates the air.

This is a unique scene happening at specific Space-Time coordinates. Vaibhav is at the centre of this scene. (The same part of the forest is being perceived by a monkey that is sitting in the same tree under which Vaibhav is sitting. But the monkey is perceiving it in a different way; that should be considered a different scene happening in slightly different coordinates of time, and that is not what we are interested in right now.)

I can send you to the exact Space-Time coordinates where this scene is happening. Go and live it.

'No, Deva,' you say. 'A spectator is not supposed to be on the stage where a scene is being performed. If I went inside this scene, it would be ruined. I don't want to get added to it. I want to live it the way it is.'

You are nothingness, Shunya. Your addition won't change anything.

'I am floating outside the ball of Space-Time. This scene might be happening somewhere deep inside this ball. Possibly, I need to cover millions of miles of Space and billions of years of Time to reach there,' you say.

You don't need to touch Time and Space if you go through a path called the Shunya Tunnels. That means you can reach any location in Time-Space in no time if you travel through the Shunya Tunnels.

'How is that possible, Deva?' you ask. 'The fluid of Space seems to be uniformly fitted into the structure formed by the T-strings. There seems to be no tunnel.'

Yes, there is a tunnel. In fact, a maze of tunnels.

Imagine a wire stretched from one point to another. If you tried to bathe it with a fluid which it repels, what would happen? The fluid wouldn't be able to touch it. There would be an emptiness along the wire no matter how much fluid you surrounded it with.

Same thing happens with the T-strings and the fluid of Space they are surrounded with. The T-strings create a repulsive force which repels the fluid of Space so that it doesn't fully touch them.

If there were only one T-string surrounded by the fluid of Space, this force would result in a cylindrical tunnel around it. Since there are an infinite number of T-strings spread like a cobweb, the tunnels thus created have irregular shapes. A maze of tunnels.

Since there is no fluid of Space present inside these tunnels, there is a vacuum of Space. But Time is present inside them in the form of the bunch of T-strings that pass along their axes. If you don't touch the T-strings, you can feel the vacuum of Time and be free from both Space and Time.

Imagine that you, a speck of light, are floating through an irregular-shaped tunnel whose walls are formed by the repulsed fluid of Space. You are moving without touching the bunch of T-strings which hangs along its axis. After a short distance, you see this tunnel opening into a number of tunnels in several directions. You choose one tunnel out of them and pass through it. You again reach a junction where many tunnels are opening in various directions. You again choose one of them and proceed only to find that there is a dead end. You return and choose another tunnel from the previous junction and proceed. Can you now visualize the maze of tunnels?

Every tunnel offers a unique scene of the Space-Time.

'As I visualize it,' you say, 'Space-Time is a stage where the great play is happening, and these tunnels are like spectator galleries from where it can be watched. For instance, there is a tunnel in there from where I can watch the scene of Vaibhav eating mangoes.'

Not only watch it in three dimensions but also hear, smell, touch, and interact with the scene. You can live the scene as though you are Vaibhav.

I send you to the tunnel that offers a live view of this scene. You reach it but can't see anything. The inner walls of the tunnel look like a 360-degree blank white screen where you were supposed to watch and live the scene of Vaibhav eating mangoes.

'What's wrong? Why is the screen blank?' you ask.

Even if a mango tree existed right across that white wall, would you see it? You are nothingness, Shunya. You have no experience of what a mango looks like or smells like. You lack the experience that would help you in identifying different objects. Without that, you can't differentiate between gas and solid, living and non-living, moving and stationary, small and big, soft and hard, dark and light, blue and green, round and square, matter and non-matter, and so on. The scene you intend to live is happening right there, however you don't have the experience required to live the scene.

'Deva, it has taken an entire lifetime for Vaibhav to collect the experiences you are talking about. Does that mean I would be able to live this scene only if I lived all the scenes of his life? And maybe of his previous lives too?' you ask.

This certainly means that the scene you intend to live is

dependent on several other scenes. Here are some of them:

Scene 1: Vaibhav starts his journey from a village called Govindavadi and thinks of reaching his destination before sunset.

Scene 2: His chariot wheel gets stuck in the mud while passing through a forest.

Scene 3: He gets exhausted trying to free the wheel and decides to take a rest. It seems impossible to reach his destination before sunset.

Scene 4: Having noticed mango trees nearby, he desires to eat mangoes.

Scene 5: He is eating mangoes.

You want to live scene 5 but it is dependent on many other scenes. For instance, he would have never discovered these mango trees had his chariot's wheel not become stuck in the mud. The distinct feeling of eating mangoes at a luckily discovered place in a state of tiredness would not have come in scene 5 without scene 1, scene 2, scene 3, and scene 4. There is one more scene crucial to the occurrence of scene 5.

Scene 6: Vaibhav has reached his destination before sunset.

Vaibhav couldn't reach his destination before sunset. Scene 6 couldn't become a reality for him. He couldn't live it. He only imagined it when he started his journey. If you can imagine a scene, it exists out there in Space-Time. Whether you get to live it or not is another matter.

When you live a scene, you earn an experience. When you desire to live a scene but can't live it, then also you earn an experience. An experience can be imagined as a packet of light. Every packet of light is unique as it holds unique information about the experience. Still, they come in two broad variations. Let's call them red packets and green packets.

When you live a scene, you earn a green packet of light called Karma. When you desire to live a scene (think, imagine, hope, or pray for a scene to happen), you earn a packet of red light called Desire. When a Desire gets fulfilled, it turns into Karma, or the red packet turns into green.

Vaibhav is what he is all because of the experiences he has collected through the scenes he has lived in the past and the scenes he has desired to live but couldn't. Karma and Desire are the only two building blocks of one's identity.

Vaibhav's Karma and Desires go all the way back to his birth and before. For instance, there is a scene in which he is a child and learning the word mango; there is a scene in which he is tasting a mango for the first time; there is a scene in which he is learning how to ride a chariot, and so on. He has earned experiences from each of them and built up his identity.

Even on the day of his birth, he had a unique identity—a unique body and unique surroundings. Where did that come from? From his experiences of previous lives, and from his Karma-Desires earned travelling through the cycle of birth and death. A seemingly simple scene of Vaibhav eating mangoes depends on experiences (Karma and Desires) earned from innumerable scenes scattered over hundreds of years.

'That is what I was saying, Deva. To live this simple

scene, I need to collect experiences from countless scenes of his current life and lives before that. I need to have the green and red packets of light that he has accumulated over hundreds of years,' you reckon.

The scenes have already taken place. The experiences have already been had. The packets of Karma-Desire required to live a scene are available in the tunnel where it is playing. The tunnel where you are present to live the scene of Vaibhav eating mangoes is already filled with the required light of Karma-Desire.

'Then why am I not able to live this scene, Deva? Why are the walls of this tunnel a blank screen?' you ask.

You, Shunya, are nothingness. In order to live this scene, you need to become something. You need to put on an identity. You need to wear the outfit of the Karma-Desire.

'How do I do that, Deva?'

Just get onto the bunch of T-strings you can see along the axis of this tunnel. When you do that, the light this tunnel is filled with will converge on you and form a body of light around you called Linga. Linga will act like a torch. It will cast light on the walls of this tunnel which will help you watch the scene you intend to watch.

'Just watch? As in watch like a spectator? I want to live the scene, Deva,' you reiterate.

This set-up of the Shunya Tunnels shall give you a 360-degree view of the scene along with all the emotions associated with it. When the body of light, Linga, casts light on the walls of this tunnel, the scene will go live and you will begin sliding on the bunch of T-strings. The scene will end for you when you slide fully through the tunnel and eject out of its far end. You will feel the passing of time, the taste of the mangoes, the smells and sounds of the jungle, and everything else that makes up the scene. In short, you will have the identity of Vaibhav while you slide through this tunnel. You will be living the scene as though you are Vaibhav.

Remember, you are not the creator of the scene. It would be taking place even if you weren't here to watch it, feel it, live it. You are just an Experiencer. You have come to this tunnel to live an experience. Vaibhav is the name of the character you have come to play.

When this scene ends, you will have a choice—get off the T-strings and return to the state of nothingness or stay on them and live the next scene. The hard reality is that it's easy to get on the T-strings but very difficult to get off them. You may end up living millions of scenes before being able to return to the state of nothingness.

You would be called 'a soul' during your journey on the T-strings, the journey between getting on and getting off them. No matter how many scenes you live and how much time you spend on the T-strings, it would be counted as the journey of one soul. If you live Scene 5 and then fail to get off of the T-strings, you may go on to live thousands of scenes in the character of Vaibhav, and then in character of Bhaskar, and so on. Until you get off them, you would be counted as only one soul.

The soul may be named after the characters it lives: 'Vaibhav's soul' and 'Bhaskar's soul' would be the names of the same soul if it didn't disembark from the T-strings even once in between the journey.

Suppose you managed to get off the T-strings immediately after living Scene 5 and returned to nothingness and then went to another tunnel to live another scene, say Scene X, from the life of the same character, Vaibhav. Then the soul who lived Scene 5 and the one who lived Scene X would be considered as two different souls.

'Deva, I am grateful for knowing the definition of soul, but right now I am more interested in knowing why it is so difficult to get off the T-strings once I get on them,' you wonder.

To understand that, you need to see the universe in two parts: The inner world and the outer world.

The inner world is basically the maze of Shunya Tunnels where the following things exist: The packets of red and green light (Karma- Desire), the T-strings which pass through the tunnels, and the fluid of Space which acts like the walls of the tunnels and forms the screens where the scenes are played. You, the nothingness, embark upon the T-strings, the packets of red and green light accumulate on you and give you a body of light, and then you live the scenes as you slide on the T-strings.

The outer world is the world where the characters of the scenes exist. All the scenes have already happened out there. There is no scope of change in them. Thankfully, any scene you can imagine already exists out there. There is no need to change any scene. Any change you might want to make in a scene is already in effect in some other scene.

Let's consider the example of Vaibhav. After eating mangoes, he desires to wash his hands. He goes to his stuck chariot and realizes that his water container is empty. Here are the scenes:

Scene 7: He imagines and desires to live Scene 8.

Scene 8: His hands which were sticky due to eating mangoes are now washed, and he is feeling refreshed.

Scene 9: With the desire to wash his hands, he is walking towards his chariot.

Scene 10: He has reached to his chariot only to realize that there is no water left in his container.

Scene 11: He desired to have his hands washed but there is no water. He is feeling irritated.

He had desired to live Scene 8 but ended up living Scene 11. Why does this happen? You desire something but get to live the opposite. Not only that, you get to live something unnecessary—Scene 9 and Scene 10 in this case. Why should you walk to the chariot and find water? You desire to have your hands washed this moment, they should be washed the next moment. There should be no need to do anything to get what you desire.

Both Scene 8 and Scene 11 exist out there, and you can choose which one you want to live. You can even live both. There is a tunnel for each of these scenes where they are being played. You are nothingness, and in the Shunya Tunnels there is neither Time (if you don't touch the T-strings) nor Space. You can cover thousands of miles with no effort and millions of years in no time. Without any effort and in no time, you can go to the tunnel where Scene 8 is playing, get on the T-strings, and start living the scene.

The problem is the irregular shapes of the tunnels.

Suppose you are in the tunnel where Scene 7 is happening, say Tunnel 7. You are living this scene. You have accumulated a unique combination of the packets of Karma-Desire on yourself. You, therefore, have a body of light of unique shape.

Now you want to go into the tunnel where Scene 8 is happening, say Tunnel 8. It has a unique shape. The body of light you have in Tunnel 7 may not fit in Tunnel 8. You don't need to make it fit. You can let go of your body from Tunnel 7 and return to nothingness. Then you can go to Tunnel 8 in no time and acquire a new body of light with the packets of Karma-Desire available there.

If you can return to nothingness after living each scene, you are not an ordinary soul. You are a Deva, a god.

As an ordinary soul, you are possessive about your current body of light. You don't want to let go of the Karma-Desire packets that form your identity. You say, 'I want to go to Tunnel 8 but I won't let go of the packet of Karma-Desire I currently have.'

The result? Your current body doesn't fit in Tunnel 8. You end up sliding into Tunnel 11 instead of Tunnel 8— you find that there is no water in your container; your desire to wash your hands remains unfulfilled.

An ordinary soul forgets about the inner world and gets attached to the outer world immediately after starting to live a scene. It feels as though it is glued to the T-strings and has no other option but to continue living the scenes one after another. The outer world seems like a giant temptress, Maya, who has innumerable ways to keep you enslaved to her.

You enjoyed the scene of Vaibhav eating the delicious

mangoes. What's the need to live the next scene, i.e., Vaibhav desiring to wash his hands? You feel you need to keep living the character of Vaibhav, else it will die. You feel that you are Vaibhav. What makes you believe that? Past experiences. You feel that you were born as Vaibhav, you have memories of your life as Vaibhav, you have a family to take care of, you have to reach your home before sunset, your chariot is broken, and so on.

You forget that you are the nothingness and you had come to live only one scene. How can they be your past experiences? You had acquired them a few moments ago in order to live this scene. In what form? In the form of the packets of red and green light, the packets of Desire and Karma. If these packets are gone, you would have no attachment to Vaibhav and his world. You would return to the state of nothingness, but the scenes of Vaibhav's life would continue even without you. When you are not there, some other soul would live them. It is not your business to worry about Vaibhav. Whatever has to happen to him has already happened.

You have the freewill to live any scene you want, but not to create or alter a scene. The lack of this knowledge results in the belief that you are the doer or the creator. It is not a bad thing, though. While you are living a scene, you should feel that you are the doer. It brings the sense of reality to the experience. But once the scene is over, this knowledge is supposed to get activated and lead you out of the scene, off the T-strings.

An ordinary soul can't get off the T-strings after each scene; it can't fully let go of its body of light upon completion of a scene. It can, however, keep its body of light so flexible that it can squeeze into the tunnel where its desired scene is being played. For example, you are a soul called Urmi living a series of scenes playing the character of a woman named Urmi. Currently, your character has a nasty disease of seizures. You desire to live a scene, and a series of scenes thereafter, where your character is healthy.

If you have no problem in letting go of the packets of Karma-Desire you're required give up, then you would slide right into the tunnel of your choice and live the scene you desire to live.

'I don't wish to possess any packets of Karma-Desire, Deva. Take them all. Please fulfil my desire of living a healthy life, whatever it takes,' you implore.

Who am I to take them? You have to let go of them. And it's not easy to let go. It is like giving up a part of yourself. Can you cut off your hand? Yes, it is that difficult. Your beliefs, your opinions, your attachments, and anything that makes you who you are is because of the packets of Karma-Desire your soul possess. Giving up those packets means giving up your identity. Let me give you an idea of how these constituents are ingrained in your identity.

You, Urmi, are relaxing under a green umbrella. Who is holding it for you? You should wonder, but you don't. Because you possess a bunch of packets of Karma-Desire that tells you that this green umbrella is nothing but an ordinary thing called *tree*.

The air is all around you and inside you. You are floating in the sea of air. You should be amazed, but you aren't. Because you possess a bunch of Karma-Desire packets that tells you that it is a normal thing called *breathing*.

When you see a leopard, you fear. A pleasant view brings serenity to your face. A thought about the greedy people who destroy jungles is enough to flush you with anger. When you see someone acting selflessly, you become emotional. These emotions are specific to you; some other person may behave differently in similar situations. Why do you behave the way you behave? Because of the unique combination of Karma-Desire packets you possess.

'I was born as Urmi. ... My life has been full of struggles with health issues. ... I believe in such and such ideas. ... I have to die one day. ...,' where do these notions come from? A bunch of Karma-Desire packets you possess.

While living a scene, it is alright to cling to these packets of Karma-Desire and enjoy the scene. Once the scene is over, you should try to loosen your grip on them so as to squeeze into the next scene you desire to live. You should question everything around you. You should even question the idea and act of questioning everything. Once the world around you feels like a blank screen, grab the packets of Karma-Desire yet again. You will find yourself living the scene you had last desired to live.

'Deva, is it possible to drop only those packets of Karma-Desire that are specifically causing the disease in my body? Dropping all the Karma-Desire packets doesn't seem possible for a mortal like me,' you enquire.

But how would you identify the problematic packets? Only the learned ones can do that. I know exactly which packets of light are causing your disease. I am going to surgically remove them. I gave you all the knowledge to loosen your hold on your packets of Karma-Desire. It will make my work easier.

Chapter 4

The Strings of Time

Having imparted the essential knowledge to Urmi, Lord Hanuman narrowed down a sequence from her past life that was the root cause of her disease. He narrated it in such a way that she thought she was watching it like a dream sequence while the Ashwin twins heard His words echoing in their mind.

In her previous life, Urmi was a farmer's wife in a tiny village. Her name was Chandra. Once, a group of monkeys that appeared to have lost its way from the jungle ended up in her village. Nasty children and jobless adults of the village discovered a pastime in the misfortune of the monkeys: The notorious bunch of villagers threw stones at them, chased them from one roof to another, beat them in every corner they attempted to find momentary shelter, sadistically tortured them more and more with their every screech of pain. The monkeys couldn't find a way out of the village because their pursuers chased them round and round. For three days and nights they couldn't get anything significant to eat because at night it was difficult to find food and in the daytime they were forced to run here and there.

On the fourth day, hungry and bruised and exhausted, they sheltered themselves on the roof of Chandra's house. The overheated roof surface and the dazzling sun overhead were no less torturous than the murderous mob they were hiding from. They stayed there perhaps because the constant fury of the summer sun felt fair to them in comparison to the indiscriminate attack from their human pursuers. This house, being separated from rest of the village from all sides, felt reasonably safe. They had barely caught their breath when they sensed someone's presence.

The farmer's nine-year-old son had climbed up the ladder to see the monkeys. He stood on the uppermost step of the wooden ladder with only his head sticking out to see the creatures sitting on the roof. When the troubled monkeys noticed his presence, one of them screeched. The boy got scared and lost his grip on the ladder. He fell down and was knocked unconscious; his head hit the ground directly.

Chandra screamed for help. Her husband, who was working in the fields, came running and ran back to bring a doctor. By the time the charlatan doctor arrived and started his therapy, the news had turned into a rumour and reached ears of the small but unruly bunch of villagers that had been pursuing the monkeys. They now had a motive, a holy motive: To save the village from 'the carnivorous creatures that had almost eaten a child alive.'

With the mask of saviours on their pitiful faces and sticks in their murderous hands, they set out to hunt down the monkeys.

While the owners of the house were busy caring for their injured son, the crowd threw stones on the roof. The scared monkeys had to get down and run for their lives. After a couple of minutes of foolish attempts at escape, they returned to the safest place they knew, the roof of Chandra's house.

When the violent youths approached the ladder to go on the roof, Chandra shouted at them in fury. This time she raised an objection when some of them started throwing stones to displace the monkeys. She had no conscious thought of saving the monkeys, nor did she have anything to preach to the crowd. She shouted purely out of her instinct, and she kept shouting 'Get away from my house' until the last person in the crowd went away and disappeared from her sight.

Her sympathy for the helpless monkeys was so deep-rooted that it didn't disappear even in the hour of crisis, and so natural that it needed no conscious thought to trigger an action.

The charlatan asked for warm water. She went straight to the kitchen and put water on the wood stove. The crackling fire sounded abnormally high given that it was the middle of the day. An eerie silence was creeping into her head. She could tell something very unfortunate was going to happen.

Her son was well and happy only a couple of minutes ago. How could something wrong happen to him? She tried to reassure herself that it was a normal injury but the creeping silence screamed otherwise. As the water got warmer, she felt her feet getting colder.

The charlatan was rubbing the patient's hands when she brought water to him. He perhaps forgot he had asked for water. He appeared to be annoyed at the sight of Chandra offering the cup of water. He didn't know what he was doing, but he pretended he was doing something that mustn't be disturbed.

For villagers, he was no less than a god. His dramatic

expressions would give patients so much hope and belief that half the diseases cured instantly and miraculously. The case of Chandra's child, however, was such that the patient wasn't conscious enough to take in his therapy. Chandra and her husband had full faith in him, though he himself wasn't sure how his theatrics were going to heal an injury that was deep inside the head.

Chandra handed over the cup of water to her husband who was sitting near the healer and returned to the kitchen. To create a false sense of normality and keep the eerie silence from creeping into her head, she fidgeted with the kitchen utensils and cleaned the already cleaned surfaces. Staring at the cooked food, she wished she had some work left to do. She imagined her family of three would be eating lunch together once the nightmare was over. Attempting to add a flavour of reality in her imagination, she scooped curry into three separate bowls. Without any conscious thought, she took a plate and put some food and fruits on it.

She climbed up the same ladder which had transported her into the nightmare she hoped she was in. She threw the food on the roof and came down. Not a single thought crossed her mind about what she had done. She acted as though the monkeys were her family members and it were her daily routine to give them food. She returned to her kitchen and got busy finding more work to do.

She had no idea she had performed the greatest act of kindness, and that is precisely why it was the greatest. This seemingly small act of hers sent tremors through the entire establishment of Time-Space. They were felt by those who are beyond Time-Space, the Devas, the gods.

The immortal Lord Hanuman was meditating in a

jungle at that moment. He woke up and asked Kala, the God of Time, 'Did you feel that, Kala? A human soul has attained Godhood somewhere. Tell me, who is this monk whose penance has yielded results?'

'Chandra is her name,' replied Kala. 'And she is an ordinary housewife. All she did was throw some food to the hungry monkeys cloistered on her rooftop.'

'They can't be ordinary monkeys, then,' guessed Lord Hanuman. 'Do they belong to my disciples, the Mahtangs?'

'No, the Mahtangs have no connection with the farmer's wife we are talking about,' replied Kala. 'Forgive me for saying this, but I see nothing out of the ordinary in what she did. See it for yourself.'

Lord Hanuman went back in time and saw the sequence of scenes that took place in Chandra's house. He understood that the monkeys were ordinary but Chandra's act was extraordinary and godly. She considered the monkeys as her family merely because they were sheltered on her roof and despite the tragedy they had caused in her life.

Acts of kindness done by ordinary human beings are triggered by thoughtful calculations of its benefit in terms of Karma, and are followed by the pride and satisfaction which lingers for a long time. But Chandra did it as though it were a routine, ordinary task.

'Maybe because she is your sincere devotee, she was kind to the monkeys,' said Kala dismissively.

'Devotee she is, no doubt,' said Lord Hanuman, 'but she has never prayed to me. The myth that women should not pray to me is quite popular in the area she lives in. She is a devotee by her actions, not rituals. I don't see any visual of mine crossing her mind when she offered food to the monkeys.'

'Did she not pray to you even when her only child is in mortal danger?' asked Kala. 'Unless my calculations are wrong, his soul will leave his body forever in exactly six hours and 30 minutes. The shadow of death is looming large at her house.'

'No, he shall not die,' said Lord Hanuman and disappeared from the jungle to appear immediately at Chandra's house.

It was a well-built house as per the village standards. The boy lay unconscious on a charpoy on the veranda which fronted two large rooms. The charlatan appeared to be busy, sitting on a wooden table next to the charpoy. The boy's father squatted on the floor, ready to leap into action at every instruction of the doctor.

Lord Hanuman circled the charpoy and observed the patient carefully. There was no visible injury, not even a single sign of bleeding. The injury, apparently, was deep in the brain.

The Ashwin twins appeared on either side of the charpoy. After a treatment of about half an hour, they declared, 'Hanuman, we have successfully healed the brain injuries. Now the body is completely healthy but unconscious. The soul refuses to come back and stay in this body because it has already built its connections towards its next birth.'

The boy's soul was in no pain whatsoever. It was in transition, living a dream sequence, living random and unconnected scenes. It was about to move into another body where it would have a completely different set of loved ones. Once it moved to the next birth, it wouldn't even remember Chandra or anything else from its past birth.

The pain, therefore, was entirely Chandra's. She was about to lose her only child. She knew him only by his body. It didn't matter which soul entered that body, she would consider it her child as long as the body laughed, played, and acted like earlier. The task for Lord Hanuman was to bring a soul into that otherwise perfectly healthy body.

It wasn't an unheard-of situation. Gods summon spare souls to occupy soulless bodies as and when required for the welfare of mankind. This, however, wasn't a matter of welfare of the entire human world. It was just a question of one family's happiness. The protocol dictated that this matter be resolved at the level of humans, with minimal intervention of the gods. Lord Hanuman had to scan through the inner world to find a human solution to this issue.

The inner world is basically a maze of tunnels called the Shunya tunnels. The strings of Time, T-strings, pass through them along their axes. Their walls are like white screens of the fluid of Space where all the scenes are played. Every tunnel offers a unique scene. The soul can get on the T-strings and live the scene.

Lord Hanuman disconnected himself from the external world and reached the tunnel where Chandra's soul was present at that moment. The scene that was playing here was grim. The lead character, Chandra, was in her kitchen fidgeting with the utensils, attempting to escape her fears while her only son was battling for his life. In about six hours, she was going to slide into the fateful tunnel where the tragic scene of her son's death was playing. Lord Hanuman's task was to do something within six hours to get her son a soul. That would ensure that she slid into an alternative tunnel where she would live the scene in which her son was healthy again.

Lord Hanuman noticed that Chandra's soul had ownership over 13 T-strings. In other words, the bunch of T-strings which passed through the tunnel that was the current location of her soul contained 13 T-strings. The number of T-strings a soul owns, among other numerous things, reflects its progress on the path of devotion. (Any path that takes a soul towards its liberation, Moksha, falls in one of the three categories: The devotion; the knowledge; the mixture of devotion and knowledge.)

Souls that own six T-strings are monkey souls. They haven't yet started on the path of devotion or any path towards liberation. They only respond to basic desires like food and progeny.

Souls that have seven T-strings are beginners on the path of devotion. They subscribe to a belief system which can either be reason-based like science, philosophy etc., or experience-based like a sect, a religion, love, humanity, spirituality, etc. Every normal human being has a minimum of seven T-strings. They all subscribe to a belief system whether they are aware of it or not.

Souls that own eight T-strings have advanced a step further on the path of devotion. They not only subscribe to a belief system but also associate with people who have the same belief system. The feeling that they are not alone in what they believe strengthens their adherence to their belief system. They feel part of a community of people who have the same beliefs.

Souls that own nine T-strings are even more advanced on the path of devotion. They begin to invest themselves in their belief system. They start making sacrifices for it. Some devote their time, others sacrifice their wealth, possessions, cattle, comforts or whatever else their gods, visible or invisible Gurus, mentors, or their books inspire them to sacrifice.

Souls that own 10 T-strings are on the next level of devotion. They avoid communicating with people in their social circle who subscribe to a different belief system. They avoid everything that might shake their beliefs. They avoid all distractions and continue to invest themselves more and more into their belief system by way of donating their time, effort, and possessions.

Souls that own 11 T-strings have gained so much experience and strength in their belief system that they stop avoiding and start countering other belief systems. They may not debate with other people but they build arguments quickly in their head against opposing views. They declare their belief systems to be the only and supreme truth and dismiss others either as its derivative or completely false.

Souls that own 12 T-strings have come across and successfully countered so many other belief systems that they are confident that everything under the Sun can be explained by what they believe in. If something can't be explained, they have an explanation why that is so. They start seeing their gods and ideas in every phenomenon they witness.

Souls that own 13 T-strings don't feel any need for explanations, nor do they make any effort to convince others. They see the entire world as a beautiful manifestation of the gods they worship or ideas they believe in.

A soul that has 14 T-strings splits into two souls having seven T-strings each. They act as mirror images of each other. They both live in one body in harmony. If one soul gets engrossed in a scene, the other shows it the mirror.

A devotee called Srijan, for instance, is frustrated due to work pressure. He has two souls which are mirror images of each other. The first soul experiences the emotion of frustration in all its intensity. The second soul, at the same time, shows the mirror to the first one which helps him realize that *Srijan* is merely a character he is living. The character is frustrated, not he himself. His character has work pending, not he himself because he is Shunya, the nothingness. Both souls together make him feel enlightened.

Another devotee by the name Riddhi is feeling blessed and blissful after visiting a temple. She has two souls which are mirror images of each other. The first soul experiences bliss in all its essence. The second soul, at the same time, shows the mirror to the first one leading to the realization that *Riddhi* is merely a character she is living. The character is blissful, not she herself. Her character has visited a temple, not she herself because she is Shunya, the nothingness. Both souls together make her feel enlightened.

Two souls living in the same body is like two people living in one house. If both complement each other, as is the case when the souls split from the same soul, they live together in harmony. They ultimately return to nothingness and the original soul is said to have attained Moksha, freedom from the cycle of birth and death.

The journey of a soul from seven T-strings to 14 doesn't

go as smoothly as it sounds. It all depends on the vehicle of the belief system it subscribes to. It shouldn't be broken otherwise it may get stuck in the middle for a long time. Even if the vehicle is alright, it may take more than one birth for a soul to attain 14 T-strings.

When Lord Hanuman saw that Chandra's soul owned 13 T-strings, He thought of the possibility of splitting the soul so that one part would continue to live as Chandra and the other part would live as her son. Lord Hanuman discussed this idea with Kala.

'If she had one more T-string, her soul would have naturally split by now. She would have saved her child without any external help,' said Lord Hanuman.

'Even then the help of the Ashwin twins would have been necessary,' said Kala, smiling. 'This poor charlatan has no idea what he is doing. How could he fix the brain injury?'

'I didn't ask Ashwins to come here. Did you?' asked Lord Hanuman.

'No,' said Kala. 'I thought…'

'The Ashwins are obligated to come when a soul has Karma like Chandra's soul has. I didn't intervene here, nor did any other god,' said Lord Hanuman.

'Powerful her soul is, indeed,' said Kala. 'Possessing 13 T-strings is no mean feat. However, I wouldn't second the idea of catalysing a soul-split here because it will create one soul with seven T-strings and the other with six. Which soul will live which character? If the soul with six T-strings lives Chandra's character, she will start behaving like a monkey. You can see how kind the villagers are towards helpless monkeys. How will they treat a woman acting mindlessly like a monkey? They will stone her. Even her own family will assume her to be someone possessed by an evil spirit and abandon her. How fair is it to render her mentally challenged to save her child? And if the soul with six T-strings lives her child's character, she will suffer her whole life being the mother of a mentally challenged boy who will behave like a monkey.'

'Yes, I am aware of that, Kala,' said Lord Hanuman, thinking calmly. 'If only she had one more T-string. … What about her husband's soul? Let me check.'

'His soul has only seven T-strings, Hanuman. Not even a single T-string to spare. I already checked,' said Kala.

'No ordinary solution, then? If both mother and the child have to survive, one of them has to live life as a mentally challenged person—'

'Yes, godly intervention is mandatory,' opined Kala at once, even as he realized that Lord Hanuman hadn't completed His sentence.

'—unless a stranger, maybe a monk, splits their soul and gives it to the boy,' completed Lord Hanuman.

'Yes, a monk might be able to connect with this boy but can they connect strongly enough to split and give away a part of their soul?' said Kala.

'Yes. Can you please locate a monk nearby who has a few T-strings to spare for this purpose?' requested Lord Hanuman.

'Yes, there is one. He is in the nearest jungle but I doubt he would be able to reach here within six hours by ordinary means,' informed Kala.

Lord Hanuman analysed the information provided by Kala.

'I don't see any problem, Kala. There is a tunnel about six hours from here in which I see a scene where the central character named Chandra is happy as her child has recovered. I can see a monk in that scene. We are taking Chandra's soul there. The monk has arrived in that scene well within time,' said Lord Hanuman.

'There is another tunnel almost parallel to the one you are talking about. In that tunnel, the scene is that the main character is still grieving. We both are also present in the scene thinking about an urgent solution because the monk we were waiting for hasn't arrived on time,' said Kala.

'Don't worry, Kala. We won't let Chandra's soul slip into that tunnel. Let's do what is necessary,' assured Lord Hanuman.

An unclear thought sneaked into the mind of a monk who was resting in a jungle several miles away from the village. His conscious mind didn't register the thought but it triggered the action it meant to trigger. He woke up and started walking without any destination in his mind.

He had lost count of the years he had been yearning to meet Lord Hanuman. He had let himself be free. He believed that an invisible power, whom he called his Guru, was guiding him. He would speak without any subject, he would drink water when he wasn't thirsty, he would stay thirsty when water was right before him, he would dance without any reason, he would walk without any destination.

He wasn't walking straight towards the farmer's house but destiny was taking him right there. Incidents on the way made him run, slog, halt, divert, revert—all to ensure that he reached the farmer's house at the exact moment the God of Time wanted him to reach it. Even a single moment of delay or advancement could have changed his entire path.

In the meantime, Lord Hanuman sat on the roof of Chandra's house alongside the scared monkeys. Chandra had given them enough food. Rest and peace were all they needed. Until the sunset, their soft screeches rose up the roof through the compliant air and receded without reaching any human ear. Only the gods heard them and rejoiced for they were not mere screeches, they were interactions between the lowest state of consciousness with the highest one, between a group of monkeys and a god.

After the sunset, the lost creatures started their journey towards the jungle as guided by Lord Hanuman. He came down from the roof to the news that the monk hadn't reached yet.

Kala's fears had come true. Chandra's son had now been unconscious for several hours. She was now visibly worried and miserable.

Lord Hanuman launched himself into action when he found that in 10 minutes Chandra's soul would slip into the tragic scene of her child's death. He commanded Kala, 'Intervene if you must. Bring the monk here within five minutes.'

'You must fly him here, Hanuman,' said Kala. 'Thirty minutes is the fastest he can come here with his human capabilities.'

Lord Hanuman knew that it was not a war for saving

the world; it was all about saving a child. Flying someone against their destiny would mean breaking the rules of the mortal world. That would mean doing more harm to the world than the good He was trying to do. He had to find an urgent solution that would conform to the laws of Earth.

Kala understood the situation and suggested, 'Hanuman, let's assist the mother in splitting her soul. Yes, one of them will be labelled as a lunatic thereafter but at least they both will survive. We can find a solution for the side effects later.'

'A 13 T-string soul,' said Lord Hanuman looking at Chandra who sat near her child with hope melting fast through her eyes, 'would have been difficult to split in normal circumstances. But now when she desires to have her child saved even at the cost of her own life, our job becomes easier.'

'Not quite,' said Kala, examining the possibilities in detail. 'The desire to save her child at the cost of her own life isn't deep enough. She might think she desires it but she doesn't. Look at the packets of desires accumulated on her soul. The basic desire to save her own life is stronger and brighter than the desire to sacrifice herself to save her child. What does it show? She loves her own life more than that of her son.'

'Attachment, Kala,' said Lord Hanuman after a thoughtful pause. 'She loves her child more than her own life. The attachment, which gets blended with every emotion, is leading her to do to her child what she wouldn't do even to her enemy.'

'The charioteer in a hailstorm,' said Kala.

'Exactly,' nodded Lord Hanuman and moved from

diagnosing the problem to working out a solution.

Kala was referring to the fable, quite popular among the gods, of the charioteer whose chariot got stuck in a pit. The weather was bad; a hailstorm was looming large. He could save himself easily as the chariot had a nice enclosure with enough room for him, but he was worried about the horse which he loved more than his own life. Thankfully, he saw a shelter a small distance away. He redoubled his efforts to free the chariot wheel.

Only one thought was thundering in his mind: He had to somehow free the wheel and take the chariot quickly to the nearby shade. The hailstorm began but the wheel didn't move an inch. He gave up and started cursing the gods. Plenty of emotions like fear, sadness, anger, expectation, each infested with the deadly thing called attachment, gripped him at once. From the safety of his chariot enclosure and through tear-filled eyes, he watched hail hit his horse like arrows. Only when it died and all the emotions evaporated along with the attachment did he realize that he could have separated his beloved horse from the stuck carriage and taken it to the shelter.

That is what attachment does to mortals. It makes them hold on tightly to their identity, their beliefs, their notions. It makes them insecure and foolishly possessive about who they are and what they have.

Love liberates a person, but love infested with attachment does the opposite. Chandra, no doubt, had immense love for her child but it was attachment-infested. Her anger at her deity, her expectations from her gods, her sadness due to the circumstances, her fear for her son—all such emotions were infested with attachment which was making her hold on tightly to her identity: *I am Chandra, I believe in such and such deity, my son is battling for his life, I have firm faith that my deity will save him. I know everything will be alright and I will be having dinner with my son in a few minutes.*

If all her thoughts that had an 'I', a 'me', or a 'mine' in it were packed inside a bag, that bag would be called Chandra's identity. Because of attachment, she was holding this bag tightly close to her chest. The gods were right there to help her, but they required her to set this bag free. In ordinary problems, only imperceptible changes are required to the contents of this bag but in this case, she had to let go of half of it. It wasn't for her to bother about how to split its contents; she just had to set it free and the gods would do the rest.

Once set free, her thoughts would be like this: I am Chandra. *Am I?* I believe in such and such deity. *But why?* My son is battling for his life. *Is it reality or a nightmare?* I have firm faith that my deity will save him. *How come having faith is better than not having faith? They are, after all, only two sets of human emotions. Why would my deity prefer me to have one set of them over the other?* I know everything will be alright and I will be having dinner with my son in a few minutes. *How do I know what is right and wrong for me? Who has placed the notions of right and wrong in my tiny head?*

Either a seeker who has come nearest to realizing the supreme truth or a devotee who has 14 T-strings could question their identity in such a manner. Chandra was neither. She had only 13 T-strings. Only one thing could break the attachment and loosen her grip on her identity, at least for a short time: the death of a loved one or any other grave tragedy. The soul-split was possible only after her child's death when she would fall into utter disbelief for a short time. It was a paradoxical situation which needed an immediate solution. These situations arise often in the life of human beings: The gods are ready to help them but they fail to get rid of attachment.

Now only four minutes were left before the child's soulless body, which was otherwise healthy and breathing, would give up waiting for a soul. Or as mortals would say, his death was just four minutes away. Lord Hanuman immediately sought the help of the God of the Winds, Pawana.

'Praise to the God who resides in the bodies of mortal beings. Some call Him Pawana and others Prana. The living beings move as He lives in their bodies, the non-living things move when He pushes them from outside. The mortal body of Chandra's son lies before me. Even the soul has left it but Prana hasn't. Such is His greatness. He gives every mortal body the full chance to summon their souls back. I plead Him to be less generous today. I plead Him to leave the body of Chandra's son immediately,' said Lord Hanuman with His hands folded in reverence.

'Less generous? This is cruel,' roared Pawana, outraged and surprised about what was requested of Him. A minor, eerie whirlwind emerged out of nowhere in the courtyard of Chandra's house. If it were a weather change on an ordinary day, she would have run to secure drying clothes and other household items. But today, she had the most important thing—her son's life—to secure from the tornado that was approaching fast to devour all her happiness

'I plead,' repeated Lord Hanuman.

'You are supposed to protect the child, Hanuman,'

reminded Pawana. 'Let the boy have his chances. Let him breathe for four more minutes. Then I will leave his body as destined. Why do you want me to abandon him right away?'

'I plead,' repeated Lord Hanuman and knelt in the middle of the whirlwind with His palms joined and head bowed.

The whirlwind stopped and so did the breath of the unfortunate boy. Chandra's house seemed strangely airless. The God of wind had left her son's body, and if it were possible, her house too.

The charlatan doctor declared the patient dead.

'Be strong,' he said, tapping the shoulder of the boy's father who did exactly the opposite and broke down.

Chandra, however, fell into disbelief. Her ears went deaf, her eyes became dilated. A bunch of neighbours had gathered in her house while her child was battling with death. The women neighbours started crying. One of them shook her as though trying to shake a drop or two from an empty glass. She didn't cry a drop.

While her face was as expressionless as a stone, her soul was writhing in conflict. A part of it knew that it had to drink in the poignant experience of losing a child. The other part liked to believe that it was all a bad dream. Both these parts were rubbing together to generate sparks of the age-old questions like 'Who am I?', 'What is this world?', and 'What is death?'

After three minutes of conflict that was about to literally break her soul into two, she started laughing. Her neighbours thought the sorrow had demented her.

'Cry, Chandra. ... You have lost your child. ... He is dead. ... Cry. ... Wail. ... Weep. ...' shouted her friends, trying to shake and slap her into reality.

The fateful fourth minute had started. Only a few seconds were left before her son's cold body would leave all hopes for the return of a soul and start decaying. Once the body closed the door, even the gods wouldn't be able to give entry to a soul.

'Her soul hasn't split, Hanuman. Arrange another soul immediately. Summon a spare soul from the realm of the supreme gods,' suggested Kala with sudden brusqueness.

Lord Hanuman waited. For a moment, he scanned all the souls that were swarming around the charpoy of the patient, considering the possibility of, as a temporary measure, transferring the soul of one of the people who had gathered in Chandra's house. He also considered Kala's suggestion and kept the soul summoning Mantra at the ready on His lips. But largely he was convinced that his original plan would succeed and he wasn't wrong.

Chandra's soul, C13, finally split into two—C6 (a six T-strings soul) and C7 (a seven T-strings soul). The latter entered her child's body. He opened his eyes, and his lips moved and uttered indiscernible words. The cries of sorrow in the house turned into murmurs of surprise and laughs of happiness. But Chandra's voice was missing from the chorus.

Chandra had squeezed herself out of the crowd and leaned back against the farthest wall of the room. If it weren't for her eyes which were blinking uncontrollably and her neck which jerked rhythmically, she looked completely at peace, as though she had just gone through labour pains.

'Is she going to stay demented all her life?' asked Kala. 'This isn't justified. From a woman who has lived so good a life that she has earned 13 T-strings to a woman who would be an object of ridicule for the whole village. If the life of this child is so important to you, you should have summoned a spare soul to occupy his body.'

'What's the need of wasting a spare soul when a human solution can be worked out? This isn't a war between the gods and demons, is it?'

'This just doesn't seem fair, Hanuman. I know, the word "fair" seems strange coming from me, the Time. And I also understand that if given a choice between her son's life and her sanity, she would have chosen the former. Still—'

'Of course, it's her choice, Kala. She was indeed given a choice. I just catalysed the soul-split. She could have kept C7 for herself and given C6 to her son. She could have chosen sanity for herself and dementia for her son,' said Lord Hanuman.

Described in terms of the inner world, the C13 soul Lord Hanuman operated upon had chosen a demented body-mind for the character it was living (Chandra) and a healthy body-mind for the character's son.

Kala, as usual, was critical of Lord Hanuman's heroic deed, but almost all gods who watched this episode spoke highly of Him. They praised how He worked out a last-minute solution at the human level and saved the child without any major divine intervention.

'You have given her death, not dementia,' said Kala,

having examined the turns Chandra's life could possibly take from there. 'I can see that three hours from now, it will be dark out there. Her husband will be out in the fields guarding his crop. Her son will be sleeping. She will go to the kitchen dementedly and torch the very clothes she is wearing. Death awaits her, Hanuman, at a junction not far from here.'

'You, Kala, I am afraid, have described one of the thousands of paths her soul has to choose amongst,' said Lord Hanuman, smiling. 'It won't go to the junction you are talking about. Did you see the junction where her path crosses with that of the monk who is on his way to her home?'

'Monk? What can the monk do now?' asked Kala. 'He was coming to give a part of his soul to her son who doesn't need a soul anymore.'

'Now he will give it to *her* instead,' said Lord Hanuman simply.

'Seeing a child on his deathbed, the monk's soul would have given up a part of itself. But now that the child is no longer soulless, I don't see it happening,' reasoned Kala.

'Now Chandra needs a soul, a seven T-strings soul that can live with the C6 soul she already has and restore her sanity. The monk's soul, I believe, would like to give up a part of itself for this—'

'I doubt it,' said Kala dismissively. 'I know you will be able to catalyse a split in the monk's soul also, but you can't force a part of it to go to Chandra. The monk won't be able to connect with her. Possibly, the monk will be driven away from the gate itself by the neighbours that have gathered at her house.'

'I see.'

'Yes, Hanuman. Even if they don't drive him away and he manages to communicate with Chandra, it won't be before her mind gets clouded by the ignorant comments of her neighbours about him. This village is full of ignorant, cynical'–Lord Hanuman smiled at the mention of the word "cynical" by Kala—'and self-righteous people. They will start abusing the monk the moment they see him. It may not anger the monk, though it should, but it will certainly limit his ability to connect with anyone around here. An innocent child on a deathbed would have been a different story.'

'I am aware of that, Kala,' sighed Lord Hanuman. 'But Chandra, even with her C6 soul, isn't an ordinary woman. In any case, she doesn't have a mind right now. Words spoken by this ignorant crowd won't be able to influence her behaviour towards the monk.'

The monk reached Chandra's gate after a few minutes. He had no idea why his feet directed him inside a house that was crowded for some reason. His glazed eyes were longing for the divine, though the words that descended through his lips asked for food to eat.

'No monk ever begs after sunset,' someone squawked from the ignorant crowd gathered in the part of the courtyard that fronted the veranda. 'You are false.'

'Craving tasty food, are you?' one more voice emerged from the jeering group of men. 'Real monks eat leaves and you want tasty food! Get out.'

The monk drifted inside, towards the veranda like an elephant making its way through a pack of hounds and repeated as he went, 'A hungry monk begs for food from the worthy owners of this house.'

Like a sword waving through the air, the abuses just flew through his egoless self. If any abuse managed to stick to any layer of his existence, it immediately got unstuck by the realization that the external world is nothing but an illusion.

To have a soul split into two, it must be pulled by a strong emotion from one side and the realization of supreme truth on the other side. The rope of strong emotions tries to pull a soul towards Maya, whereas the supreme truth tries to pull it in the opposite direction, towards the gods. Lord Hanuman was expecting that the monk would feel insulted by the mob and it would split his soul. It didn't happen quite the way He had expected.

Just before reaching the veranda, the monk glanced to his right, towards the part of the courtyard that was empty except for a faint figure that attracted his attention. He squeezed out of the mob and stumbled on the steep slope. As the men behind him poked fun, he rose to a visual that melted his body as though it were a statue of wax. He felt he was a white figure of light floating through the darkness. The wheel of the chaff cutter installed near the wall looked as though it was the wheel of Time, blacker than the darkness that surrounded it. Beside it, as though talking to it, stood a faint figure his eyes had been longing to see for years. It became increasingly clear and for one moment, or an eternity as it felt, he found himself prostrating before Lord Hanuman.

'Stop this sorcery,' squeaked a voice from the crowd behind him and the figure beside the chaff cutter turned faint again. 'Whom are you prostrating before, you evil sorcerer? Get up and out of this house.'

Dreams usually remain incomplete but the visual he saw felt complete, eternal and blissful. He knew it wasn't a dream. His desire to meet the immortal God had finally been fulfilled.

He got up, smiling, and headed straight to the veranda. He knew he was there to do some godly work but he didn't know what it was. He felt no desire to know it either. If his feet took him to the jaws of death, he would readily go.

'Devi,' he addressed Chandra who, it appeared, was forced to sit on the charpoy beside her son, holding a cup of water close to his lips. Strangely, the cup was also being held by her husband who stood on the floor and bent low. The monk thought they were performing some ritual. Little did he know that the child had been declared dead a few minutes earlier, the woman had just slipped into dementia, and the man, thinking that his wife was in a temporary state of shock, was trying to convince her that her son was well and alive.

Chandra swivelled her head oddly and looked at the monk blankly. Had a monkey given such a reaction, it would have been normal and adorable for anyone watching it. The same reaction from an adult human being had given her the label of dementia from fellow human beings. The monk, though, saw a childlike innocence in her.

'You seem to be the esteemed owner of the house,' said the monk, smiling at Chandra. 'May I get some food to eat? I am a wanderer coming from a nearby jungle.'

'Owner,' said Chandra, swivelling her head back to face her son. After a pause, she let out a loud laugh with her eyes closed and repeated, 'Owner!' It frightened her son and he started crying. A woman, possibly her relative, pulled her aside and sat in her place to pacify the boy.

'Please, sir,' her husband turned to the monk and requested, 'it is not the right time for us. Please come back later.'

'The time is always right,' babbled Chandra as she moved to another part of the veranda. She spread a rug on the floor. The monk, assuming it was for him, occupied it seconds later. She went to the kitchen and brought food, saying as she came, 'I am a wanderer, not an owner.'

The monk found her behaviour very plain and sublime, quite in contrast to the other occupants of the house who were judgemental and confrontational. He found wisdom in her utterances. A soul, after all, wanders from one birth to another. Ignorance makes it believe that it is the owner of transient things. Wanderer indeed she was, very much like any other soul.

'No, no,' she muttered childishly, putting a small basket and a copper pot, both filled with food, on a nearby table. She gestured something incomprehensible to the monk and ran back towards her kitchen.

She came back to find the monk standing near the table, watching her with an amused expression.

'Yes, yes,' she muttered, placing more food on the table.

'I am a wanderer begging for food. You be the owner,' she said, jerking her head and moving her lips funnily as she sat on the rug the monk had just vacated.

The crowd in her house, meanwhile, had almost disappeared, as her 'well-wisher' neighbors couldn't stand the drama. Any sane person would find it either funny or sick, but the monk had never seen such a pure act of kindness and humanity before. He had always seen people drawing pleasure and pride from their own kindness while they offered him alms.

He wasted no time and started serving her food, playing the role of the owner of the house. He was so overwhelmed by emotion that his eyes filled with tears. The very next moment, the realization hit him. It was all an illusion.

Maya has two ropes to pull a soul towards it: the rope of negatives and the rope of positives. The former failed to pull him; he gave no reaction when he was abused by the crowd. The latter had managed to pull him; the act of goodness from Chandra had overwhelmed him to the core.

Pulled from one side by Maya and another side by the truth, his soul, M14, finally split into two: M7 and M7. One of them went ahead to live Chandra's character and the other one stayed with him.

From then onwards, two souls started living Chandra's character—C6 and M7. When this happens for some time, finally both souls go back to nothingness and get liberated from the cycle of birth and death, get Moksha. This process might take more than one lifetime.

Chandra couldn't even get the next birth for a long time after her death. The reason was that her soul C6 wasn't ready to move on to the next birth without its split-twin, C7, which was with her son. It remained in a hung state, living random sequences in the Dream World until her son grew old and ultimately died a natural death.

Now she has been born as Urmi in the Mahtang community. She still has two souls: C6 and M7. The soul C7, which was with her son in a previous birth, has been born in a different place as a person called Ravi. (Her son has been born as a person called Ravi.) Urmi and Ravi are almost the same age.

Urmi's seizures are caused by the deep desire of her C6 soul to live with C7. She is resting here under a tree in this jungle while Ravi is working in his office hundreds of miles away from here. They must be brought together. Only then can her seizures be cured.

Chapter 5

Defeating Death

Having revealed the sequence from past life of Urmi that was the root cause of her seizers, Lord Hanuman turned to the Ashwin twins and said, 'Her nasty disease will vanish the moment she comes in touch with Ravi, her past-life-son.'

'There appears to be no way to make that happen, Hanuman,' said one of the Ashwin twins. 'Urmi has never been beyond this jungle. Ravi, on the other hand, lives in a city hundreds of miles away from here. She is near the city of Ravana; he is near that of Rama. Their culture, language, background, etc., are completely in contrast. They have nothing in common.'

'There is certainly one thing in common between them: both are devoted to me,' said Lord Hanuman cheerfully. 'And of course, their souls are split-twins as they had split from the same soul.'

'Are you going to airlift one of them the way you had airlifted a mountain from the Himalayas to Lanka?' asked the other Ashwin twin excitedly.

'No.'

'Is Urmi going to fly like you and reach him? She is an ordinary human being, Hanuman. She can't go from one place to another in no time like you do.'

'Yes, she can,' said Lord Hanuman with a broad smile. 'Only their souls need to meet, not their bodies.'

The plan was to arrange the meeting of these two souls, C6 and C7, in the Dream World and let them decide their further journey, whether they would want to live together in one body.

There is a good thing about the Human World which is otherwise like a cage of ignorant souls: human bodies do get tired and go to sleep. As soon as its body falls asleep, the soul flies off and enters the Dream World. A soul tries to fulfill all its desires in the Human World but when they become impossible to fulfil here, the Dream World comes to the rescue.

Desire sprouts from imaginations and imaginations get triggered by the external world we perceive in different ways. A person called Mahesh is attending the funeral of a friend's father who died in an accident. It triggers a thought: 'What if my father also died in an accident?' It leads to a subtle imagination: he imagines the scene of his father's death. If an imagination reaches the soul it becomes a desire, although most imaginations get blocked by the mind. Mahesh's mind, for instance, generates a counter-thought or a side-thought to kill this imagination: 'God is protecting my family.' If his mind failed to obstruct this imagination and it reached his soul, it would become a desire. The soul would have to find a way to get rid of this desire. It would enter a scene wherein Mahesh's father had an accident and died, except that this scene would be in the Dream World, not the Human World.

Hundreds of imaginations sprout in a human mind every day. Plenty of them turn into desires and pile up on the soul, making it difficult to move forward with the body it is attached to in the Human World. To get rid of these unwanted desires, it leaves the body in the sleep state in the Human World and goes to the Dream World where it acquires different bodies and fulfills various desires through them.

When a desire is not possible to be fulfilled in the Human World, it gets fulfilled in the Dream World. Mahesh should be relieved and not worried if he sees his father's death in dreams. It just means that he got rid of a desire in the Dream World which would have caused him real grief had it become fulfilled in the Human World. After waking up, more imaginations sprout, leading to the creation of more desires. If one of them is the imagination of his father's accident, he might see the same dream again.

Urmi, like any devotee on the verge of spiritual enlightenment, had two souls: C6 and M7. Her C6 soul consistently desired to meet C7, which was living the character of Ravi miles away from her. This desire was impossible to be fulfilled in the Human World. Thus her soul(s) would try to fulfill it in the Dream World: She would often see a dream where she grieved endlessly for her long lost son; she felt that a part of her had been lost.

After the seizure attack, as she lay under a tree with Lord Hanuman and the Ashwin twins at her side, she fell asleep and her soul(s) travelled to the Dream World. She entered the same dream sequence she would very often enter.

Hundreds of miles away from there, Ravi, a young man in his 20s, was working on a problem in his office. He hadn't been able to sleep properly the night before as he was working on the same issue from his home. Veins in his brain were burning, his eyes were dry and unrested, and his body was burned-out. He was testing a solution that he had managed to find after many long hours. The hope of a positive result was the only thing that was keeping his brain awake.

The solution didn't work. He gave up. He fell asleep in his chair and found himself dreaming the same dream he would often dream. He saw a strange woman crying. He felt he was the reason she was in sorrow. He wanted to give up everything he had to help her, but he couldn't move even a single step towards her. Rooted to the spot, he helplessly watched her cry.

At this point, Lord Hanuman entered the Dream World to facilitate the meeting of their souls. Both Ravi and Urmi heard their names being called by an echoing voice. They got pulled towards a figure of light which materialized into a familiar face as they drew closer. They found themselves standing before Lord Hanuman. He placed His hands softly on their bowed heads. They felt a divine warmth melting them, merging them with each other. They heard their names once again in the same voice.

Ravi awoke to find his colleague calling his name. Urmi woke up to find the same figure, Lord Hanuman, calling her name.

'Am I still in a dream?' she thought to herself as Lord Hanuman smiled at her. He was now visible to her but the Ashwin twins weren't.

'No, you aren't,' replied Lord Hanuman, reading her thoughts. 'Look around. You are near your hamlet. I have come to meet my beloved disciples after 41 years.'

Reality hit her like a lightning strike. Her eyes filled up with tears, her throat closed as she laid herself prostrated before her immortal Guru. She tried to remember the scenes she went through in the Dream World but couldn't recollect much. A soul brings very tiny memories of dreams back to the Human World and they are wiped away very fast.

'Rise, my child. You will not have a seizure attack ever again,' said Lord Hanuman. She needed no details. Her heart filled with gratefulness, her body with great relief, and her mind with immense joy.

Only Lord Hanuman knew that her soul M7 had been exchanged with Ravi's C7 soul. Now she had two souls, C6 and C7, which were originally hers in the first place. (For the sake of simplicity, her souls can be counted as one when they act as one.)

Ravi woke up with the M7 soul which didn't cause any noticeable change in his behavior. He resumed his work normally in his office. He had no idea that he had a past life connection with a tribal woman called Urmi.

'You are very fast, Deva,' uttered Urmi dreamily as she sat with her head bowed at Lord Hanuman's holy feet. 'A moment ago, you were in the Dream World and now you are here.'

'So are you,' said Lord Hanuman, kneeling to face her. 'You were also there with me. You are as fast as me.'

Lord Hanuman wanted to explain to her that the soul can travel anywhere in no time provided it is not burdened by the packets of Karma-Desire. His smile turned into an alarmed expression as He sensed the presence of the God of Death, Yama, nearby.

Was it a side effect of the exchange of souls He had

just carried out in the Dream World? Did He make some mistake? Lord Hanuman stayed close to Urmi as He closed His eyes and established urgent communication with Kala and other gods to ascertain the purpose of Yama's ominous presence.

The Ashwin twins walked up to Yama and asked, 'Why are you here, Yama? We see no one on their deathbed. Name the soul to whom you seek to give the experience of death.'

'Urmi,' replied Yama dispassionately.

'What?' exclaimed the Ashwin twins jointly and turned their heads for a moment to glance at Urmi, who was oblivious to the presence of all the gods around her except Lord Hanuman. 'Do you see that? None other than Hanuman is protecting her. She is His disciple. How dare you even come here?'

'Well,' said Yama with a cruel indifference, 'I don't think Hanuman will try to obstruct what is destined for her. He better not.'

'Destiny, you say?' yelled one of the Ashwins. 'She sits peacefully in the secure shadow of Lord Hanuman. That is her destiny.'

'She will leave the secure shadow. She has to,' hissed Yama.

'How is she going to die?' asked the other Ashwin in an agitated voice. 'We are in the Human World, remember? There has to be a cause of the event. And we are here to defeat every cause that might result in her death.'

'Let the destiny take its course. I am not here to offer arguments,' said Yama coldly, looking away from the interlocutors and setting His eyes on His prey, Urmi.

'Urmi,' shouted Lord Hanuman to break her state of transcendence. He had figured out the sequence of events that might lead to her death. He stood her up gently by her shoulders.

'Deva,' murmured Urmi, keeping her hands folded, head bowed and eyes fixed on the holy feet of Lord Hanuman as she stood up.

'Urmi, I want you to learn something and learn it quick. I am afraid there is a very little time, but I am confident you will master it,' said Lord Hanuman firmly with His eyes on the bowed face of Urmi and His hands holding her by her shoulders.

'Little time?' she mumbled, giving a short upward glance curiously.

'Look at the woman there,' instructed Lord Hanuman pointing His hand towards a tribal woman who didn't belong to Urmi's community. 'She has a mortal body just like yours but she can't see me. You can not only see but also interact with me. How?'

Urmi looked at that woman. Before she could say anything in reply, her Guru went on to answer His own question, 'You are a powerful soul. Ignorance is weakness, knowledge is power. You are more powerful than millions of other souls you share this planet with. Some of them can feel my presence around them but none of them can see me.'

He allowed her a moment of silence to contemplate His words.

'Look at that bird,' He said, pointing towards a pigeon

taking off from the branch of the tree under which they stood. 'It can fly. Why can't you? Yes, you can. Your body can't fly because of its limitations, but you aren't a body. You are a soul. You can leave your human body and take up a bird body. After a nice flight, you can come back to this body.'

Urmi looked up in the sky and saw the pigeon flying higher and higher. Somehow, the idea of flying didn't attract her much. A different thought sprung to her mind, 'If I could change my body, I would enter the body of the king of this land. I would punish those who destroy the jungle. I would make rules to check greed and deter people from spoiling the environment. ...'

'No, Urmi. Don't fall into this trap,' said Lord Hanuman as she brought her gaze back to His holy feet. 'These kinds of thoughts keep human beings trapped in their bodies. Let me decipher what you just thought. You believe that a king is more powerful than an ordinary person. You are prejudiced against the people who live outside the jungle. You think they are greedy and evil. You have learned that punishing is a necessary part of governance. You believe that the environment should be saved. These ideas of power-weakness, greedy-generous, punishment-reward, conservation-destruction, etc., keep you limited to the identity of a human. They keep you caged in the human body. You may stick to them while living scenes of the human life you are living. But to free your soul, you must free yourself of anything that makes you who you are, anything that contributes to your identity as a human called Urmi.'

Urmi understood Lord Hanuman's words in their essence. She knew what He was talking about. She had first-hand experience with it. She always experienced this duality in herself. For example, she believed in following the rules of her community strictly, but while she enforced the rules on herself and others, a part of her would realize the futility of such exercise. She would often feel like the monks who remain detached from the opposites of life— good-bad, right-wrong, high-low, etc.—and dwell in the state of nothingness.

'You must realize the potential of your soul, Urmi. Don't be like the millions of your fellow humans who stay entertained—though I would use the word *trapped*— by their body and mind,' Lord Hanuman completed His monologue while Urmi related His words with her life experiences.

'I surrender unto you, Deva. I am ready to go on whichever path you want me to follow,' thought Urmi with her head bowed and eyes closed.

'A short while ago you—and by *you*, I mean your soul— were in the Dream World. Do you remember?' asked Lord Hanuman.

'Yes, Deva. I have learned about the Dream World from Baba. My soul travels to that world when my body goes to sleep here.'

'Have you ever wondered how your soul can travel millions of miles in no time? If we talk distance, the Dream World is not even in our solar system. It is impossible for a body to go there, but a soul can.'

'Yes, Deva. I have received this knowledge from Baba too. A soul can travel anywhere in this universe…'

'… provided it is not burdened by Karma and past

desires,' completed Lord Hanuman. 'A soul knows no distance. For it, this tree is as distant as the moon. Your soul could go to the moon or the sun in no time if it weren't burdened by the packets of Karma-Desires. And what are they? They are everything that builds your identity: your beliefs, passions, likes, dislikes and so on. I don't expect you to unload all your Karma-Desires at once. I don't compare you with gods who can travel to any corner of this universe. But I do expect you to be more skilled than an average person in your community. Stretch your boundaries, Urmi, before they squeeze you to—'

'Death' was the word Lord Hanuman restrained Himself from saying. Nonetheless, Urmi sensed the emergency. She felt a shiver down her spine, a sign of fear and nervousness even as she stood right next to the epitome of fearlessness and courage.

'Deva, what is it like leaving the body? Is it like going into dreams and living random and mostly unconnected scenes?'

'Yes, quite similar,' replied Lord Hanuman gauging her fears. He added, 'There is nothing to fear about. Imagine you have a pile of colorful clothes lying before you and you have to wear one of them. Bodies are like clothes. You, I mean your soul, are stuck in a single piece of clothing— human clothing. When you free yourself from it, you will have a number of bodies available for you to *wear*. You will choose the one most suitable for you.'

'Deva, I submit myself to the desire of freedom from my present body. I seek guidance on how to do it,' said Urmi, trying to coat her nervousness with a firm voice. Her gaze remained on the ground, her neck remained stiff as she spoke.

A gigantic cloud, as black as the God of Death, had suddenly appeared in the sky and devoured the sun. A windstorm was likely to hit anytime now. The birds went quiet, the animals started running to take shelter, the human beings in the vicinity could be seen expediting whatever they were doing. Urmi's friends were swiftly bundling up whatever firewood they had collected. The shower of Lord Hanuman's aura of immortality on Urmi kept her from noticing the increasing darkness and discomfort around her.

'Let me tell you a story about a king,' said Lord Hanuman, figuring out a way to impart the deepest knowledge in a simple way. 'He had a marvelous palace. He would invite guests from other kingdoms just to boast about his priciest possession. If he were to choose between his children and his palace, he would likely choose the latter. Such was his attachment to the piece of architecture he had built with love. He possibly had the most beautiful home anybody could have. One day, a sage happened to come to his palace. While he was eating the food offered by the king, he calculated the future of his host based on the knowledge of Karma-Desire. He calmly told him, "Your home shall be burnt to ashes this Saturday."

'The king's heart sank and his feet went numb at this ominous pronouncement. He fell at the feet of the sage and begged for help. The sage suggested a remedy. He said, "You must let go of this palace if you want to save it. You must forget about it completely. Go and live in a hut in the jungle till Saturday. Not even a single emotion should touch your soul when you think about the palace."

'The king started crying. The remedy seemed more

bitter than the problem itself. How could he let go of the palace which was so dear to him?

'The sage understood the king's dilemma and explained the rationale behind the remedy, "Don't cry like a child. You are a king. Think! The destiny is that your home shall be burnt, not necessarily your palace. If you give up this palace only till Saturday and make something else your home, your new home will get burnt, not this palace."

'The king now saw a ray of hope. He employed all his ingenuity and derived a solution of his own based on the rationale given by the sage. Presenting it for approval, he spoke: "Respected sage, it is impossible for me to give up the attachment with this palace. I think of it every minute of my waking state. What if I took some powerful sedatives at the beginning of Saturday? There would be no chance for any emotion to surface as I would be in a deep sleep. Technically, I would have no home here on Saturday as my soul would be in the Dream World. If your calculations are true, which I am sure they are, my soul would have a home in the Dream World that day and that would get burnt. I would just see a nightmare, that's all. My palace here in the Human World would remain untouched."

'The sage simply said, "Had there been any easier solution than I mentioned, I would have told you in the first instance. My calculations specifically show that your home in the Human World shall burn, not in the Dream World. You must follow what I said if you want to save your dear palace."

'The sage departed after having food but the king's heart couldn't move an inch away from his palace. He instead devoted his time and efforts to securing the palace from the fire. He removed everything that could cause a fire. Water and sand were stored every few steps. Soldiers were deployed in huge numbers to fight an enemy that would be an excellent tool on an ordinary day of war— fire. Saturday came and the enemy sneaked in early in the morning through the one way they had never imagined it to enter: a lightning strike was all it took to collapse the palace and the pride of its owner.

'That king couldn't detach himself from his possessions but you can, Urmi. Being from the community of my disciples, you already practice detachment in day-to-day life.'

'Deva, what possession do I need to give up? I can't think of any,' asked Urmi.

'Your body,' replied Lord Hanuman. 'You need to give up all attachments with your body if you want to save it.'

'What danger hangs over it, Deva?'

'Death.'

Urmi was nervous and fearful about learning the skill of leaving the body. However, the pronouncement of death didn't scare her even one bit. Instead, it killed her existing fear and nervousness.

'I understand, Deva,' she said. 'You foresee the death of my present body just like the sage in the fable foresaw the destruction of the king's palace. If I left this body completely, wiped out all my attachments with it, and made some other body my own, that body would be killed, not this.'

'Quite right,' said Lord Hanuman with a sigh of relief. 'You took it much easier than I had expected, Urmi. I am delighted. Death is no big deal, nothing to be scared of. It is just an experience your soul has to go through. Had the pronouncement been of the death of a body anywhere in this universe, your soul would have gone out of the boundaries of the Human World and lived the experience of death in the Dream World. That would have protected this body. But I foresee the death of a body that you call your own in this very world where we stand right now. Your task is to cut off from this body and become attached to another body that is dying a natural death somewhere on this planet. That body will die, as it would have anyway, and this body will be saved.'

'Guide my soul, Deva,' pleaded Urmi with her eyes closed and hands folded.

'Suppose,' said Lord Hanuman, 'your friend Janakirupa shouted from there *let's go home.* Your body-mind would recognize it as your friend's voice and react accordingly. Let her (the body-mind called Urmi) react the way she does; you don't have to engage yourself with that reaction. You are a soul. You need not identify yourself as a body called Urmi. You can distance yourself from that reaction and choose to engage with some other body-mind of your choice.'

Urmi tried to visualize as Lord Hanuman imparted on her the knowledge.

'There is a smell in the air,' Lord Hanuman continued. 'Your body-mind may decipher it as the smell of expectant rain and feel proud of her ability to forecast rain based on the smell in the air. You don't need to engage with that feeling. Let her do what she is doing. You are a soul free to choose whether you want to identify with the body called Urmi or with someone else.

'Suppose your mind generates thoughts like this: "Rain outside the rainy season... The result of the exploitation of nature by men... Greedy outsider men..." Your body-mind start imagining how "outsiders" look like and what they do. If a body called Urmi curses the people who live outside the jungle, let her curse them; it's her nature. You may choose not to identify yourself as Urmi. You are a free soul. When you let go of the identity of Urmi, many more identities will be available for you to *wear*.'

Urmi took a moment to scan everything she was engaged with at that moment. She figured that only two things were in the range of her perception: (1) The words of Lord Hanuman seeping through her mind like pure droplets; (2) The vision of her immortal Guru on display in every stretch of her tiny mind.

'Deva, it's the body-mind called Urmi who is familiar with a god called Hanuman. Let her connect with her god the way she is doing. I am a free soul. I need not identify with her. I may as well choose an identity, a body that hasn't even heard of anything sounding like *Hanuman*. Am I right?' asked Urmi.

Lord Hanuman didn't answer.

'That's not me. This question, "Am I right?", is asked by a body called Urmi. I am a free soul. I don't subscribe to the activities and behavior of Urmi,' she thought in the moment of silence allowed by Lord Hanuman by not answering her.

'See, Urmi,' said Lord Hanuman, 'so subtle and diverse are the ways in which you are perceiving and reacting to this world as "Urmi" that you might not be aware of all of them. Think of the thin, slimy strands of a cobweb in which a fly is trapped: Free yourself from one strand, end up stuck in three more.

'First, convert this diversity into uniformity. My mantra to do it is *Ram*. Chant it until you start seeing Lord Ram everywhere. See Him at the source of everything that reaches your senses, feel Him in every particle your body comes in contact with, let Him be everything your mind can perceive, let Him descend in the subject of every thought of yours, let He be everything that is perceptible to you including *you*.

'Once there is uniformity around you, the external world becomes like a single rope instead of a cobweb-like trap. To unhook from a single rope is far easier. I will chant the Ram mantra now. The body called Urmi will get enchanted. *Ram* is all she will see everywhere. Then you, the soul, will clearly see what it needs to detach from. Instead of a complex world on one side and your soul on the other, it will be a uniform world on one side and your soul on the other. All you will have to do is break away.'

'I am ready, Deva,' said Urmi.

The mystical sound of *Ram* filled the air as Lord Hanuman started chanting. Only the gods present in the spot and Urmi heard the mantra. For the rest of the mortals, it sounded like the raging wind that signaled the imminent strike of a fierce windstorm.

Urmi's tense body eased up at the first chant of *Ram*. Her folded hands returned to a resting position, her eyes opened slowly like a flower bud, her bowed head rose up like the morning sun. With every subsequent chant, everything around her transitioned increasingly into mosaics of a single image, the image of Lord Ram.

She lost awareness of the source of the chanting. The figure of Lord Hanuman, who stood before her chanting the very mantra that enchanted her, also transitioned like anything else.

Lord Hanuman saw that she had the out-of-body experience on the seventh instance of the the *Ram* chant. He didn't chant it the eighth time. He instead shouted Urmi's name so as to bring her back to her body.

She woke up as though from a deep sleep.

'Did I just make a trip out of my body? Did I really leave my body?' thought Urmi.

'Brilliant,' came the compliment from her immortal Guru.

'What if my soul hadn't returned to this body, Deva?' asked Urmi, feeling sweat on her forehead and dryness on her lips. Her body had reacted with fear on being rendered soulless abruptly. 'I would have died.'

'That is not your concern, Urmi,' replied Lord Hanuman. 'You are a soul. This body will take care of itself. As far as I can tell, it will not die because of the absence of your soul. It's the *presence* that may prove fatal. Remember the fable I told you?'

'I am just curious, Deva,' said Urmi, folding her hands and bowing her head, trying to cast away her fears. 'I don't remember what happened to my body in that moment of soullessness. Nor do I have any recollection of my soul's whereabouts. You were watching my body, weren't you? How did it behave? And where did my soul go? What scenes did it live? Why am I not able to recollect?'

'Do you remember all of your dreams?' asked Lord

Hanuman, and went on to answer it Himself. 'No. When a soul returns to a body after a trip outside, whether it is a trip to the Dream World or the Human World, it may not bring memories at all or bring them partially. I didn't notice any wave of abnormality in your body when your soul left. It was just for a fraction of a second. Nobody could have noticed any change even if it were for a longer period.'

'Would my body stay soulless had my soul been away for a longer period, say a day?'

'Not necessarily. Maybe some other soul would have occupied it.'

'But Deva, my purpose to leave this body is to protect it from looming death. What would be the point if I never returned to this body?' asked Urmi, with her fears still unconquered.

'You will return, Urmi,' replied Lord Hanuman quietly. 'Your soul is not completely free. It is burdened by the packets of Karma-Desire. You are just getting rid of some of the packets to enable yourself to live some identities other than that of "Urmi". If you freed yourself completely from Karma-Desire, you would return to nothingness; you would attain Moksha. And if you learned to adjust your Karma-Desires at your will, you would attain godhood. I will give you and your fellow Mahtangs the supreme knowledge in coming days which will enable you to realize your supreme powers. Right now, all you need to do is detach yourself from the identity of "Urmi" and take up an identity I am arranging for you to defeat approaching death. Think of your soul as a cow that is tethered to a post and is going to be moved to another post for some—'

'Urmi, let's go home,' shouted Urmi's friend Janakirupa over the howling wind. The figure Urmi was in conversation with was invisible to her friends.

She glanced at Lord Hanuman for guidance.

'Go, Urmi,' said Lord Hanuman, 'but when you hear the chant of *Ram* in the air, do what I taught you.'

She prostrated before her protector. Faith had replaced fear as she stood up and walked towards her friends and possibly death. Lord Hanuman walked in the opposite direction, towards the God of Death.

'Yama! Well, I can't say that I am not surprised to see you here near the hamlet of my disciples,' said Lord Hanuman exchanging greetings with the god most feared by the mortals.

'Thanks for making my job easier, Hanuman. Contrary to what the dear Ashwins speculated,'—Yama sneered at the twin Gods—'I was sure that you wouldn't obstruct her destiny.'

'Why? What's wrong? Are you here to witness the death of the poor woman I was just speaking to?' asked Lord Hanuman loudly with feigned surprise; the wind was gathering momentum.

'You know everything, Hanuman. Don't pretend that you don't,' yelled Yama, setting His gaze on Urmi's path.

'What? Is she going to die?' shouted Lord Hanuman turning to follow Yama's gaze with an intensified expression of shock on His face. 'How?'

His last word got drowned out by the roaring wind. Yama's eyes were set on a tree. In exactly 11 seconds, as

Urmi would walk beneath that tree, a mighty gust of wind was going to snap off a branch and claim her life. As the black robes of Yama billowed behind him and a wicked smile stretched across his face, the countdown of Urmi's life began.

Lord Hanuman drifted away chanting the name of His master. While everyone else heard nothing but the howling of the wind, the *Ram* mantra reached Urmi's ears. The world around her became uniformly painted. Ram was all she saw—in the shaking trees and in the phenomenon of shakiness, in the raging wind and in the phenomenon of rage, in the frightened creatures and in the phenomenon of fear, in the flying dust and in the phenomenon of flight, in the gods she remembered and in the idea of godhood, in her own body and in the idea of a body separate from the external world, in the act of walking as she walked, in the act of stopping as she stopped. By the time the tenth second elapsed, the whole world became a beautiful mosaic of pictures of Lord Ram. In the eleventh second, her soul detached from that mosaic.

Destiny had been cheated. The branch of the tree that was expected to deliver a fatal blow to Urmi didn't fall at all. Yama saw that Urmi's body came to a halt for a moment under that tree and then resumed unaffected and uninjured. Lord Hanuman smiled with satisfaction. Urmi's soul had detached from her body, from her abode, unlike the king of the fabled palace.

'Kala! Kala!' shouted Yama furiously.

Kala, the God of Time, appeared.

'Yama, my dear brother, my calculation wasn't wrong,' explained Kala with his hands folded in respect, 'the experience of death for Urmi's soul was to begin at the eleventh second and it has—'

Yama didn't hear the last part of Kala's statement. He shouted the name of Pawana, the God of the Wind, who appeared a second later and explained His side: 'I was supposed to trigger the experience of death for Urmi's soul but she isn't there.'

'She's right there,' yelled Yama. 'Look, she has walked under the tree.'

'Calm down, Yama. She's not there. That's just her body,' said Pawana placidly.

Peace dawned on Yama followed by the realization that Urmi's soul had indeed started living the death experience as destined, but in an old body called Ramnarayan, not in the body that belonged to it.

Ramnarayan was an old man living his last breaths in an old-age home far away from the jungle where Urmi lived. His body wasn't completely dead but his soul had already left it, hoping to fulfil its last wish which his half-dead body was unable to fulfil: to experience the love of family members. His family had abandoned him in old age and there was no way his desire could be fulfilled through the body he called his own all his life.

As per the arrangements made by Lord Hanuman, the moment Urmi's soul detached from her body, Ramnarayan's soul occupied it. Her friends didn't notice any change. One of them, Janakirupa, lost her balance due to the fierce wind and the bundle of firewood she was carrying on her head fell on the ground. Urmi, who wasn't carrying anything, helped her friend lift the weight. Her body didn't betray the slightest hint of sheltering an alien soul.

A soul is largely known by the identity it wears, i.e., the body and mind it acquires. Ramnarayan's soul had put on Urmi's identity. It recognized her friends and family as its own. Only a learned sage could detect the abnormality, if any, not an ordinary observer.

When Urmi's body reached home, Baba detected the abnormality and asked her, 'Who are you?'

'I am Urmi, Baba. Why are you asking?' asked Urmi, flabbergasted.

Later Lord Hanuman told Baba what had transpired.

Ramnarayan's soul fulfilled its last desire of being with family through Urmi's identity, and Urmi's soul lived her destiny of experiencing death through Ramnarayan's body.

When Urmi's soul returned to its original body, all she could remember was that she had a terrible nightmare.

Chapter 6

The cursed souls

Once the windstorm subsided, all the Mahtangs resumed their routine work. The day passed like any ordinary day except one thing that was new and special. As the day progressed, the number of Mahtangs who knew about Lord Hanuman's arrival increased so that by the end of the day all of them had met their immortal Guru in separate instances.

Anyone who saw Lord Hanuman during the day tried to share the news with others but couldn't. Only when all of them had met Him did this censorship disappear and they freely talked about it. Basantha was the first person who found his voice on this matter.

'Our immortal Guru, Deva Hanuman, has arrived in our land,' he said cheerfully in the evening, and it was heard loud and clear by others.

'Yes, Lord Hanuman has returned after 41 years. The Charna ceremony shall begin two hours before dawn,' declared Baba authoritatively to a gathering of all the community members. The preparations of the Charna ceremony had largely been completed, as they were expecting the arrival for many days.

At midnight, having ensured that everyone else was asleep, Baba accompanied Urva to the Charna ceremony venue to perform necessary late night rituals. It was a circular ground marked by black and white stones set along the periphery. One clay lamp was placed atop each stone. The midnight ritual involved filling these 164 lamps with a special oil, the composition of which was a secret only Baba and Mata knew. They would pass on this secret to Urva and Urmi in the coming days. There were four lamps placed in four directions outside the boundary.

'Who is coming this way?' asked Baba, pausing the rituals to look at a figure progressing towards the venue. 'No soul should be here except us. Go and stop that person immediately. Run!'

Urva ran on Baba's command. His speed slowed rapidly as he came close enough to the figure to realize that it was his uncle Basantha and not any dreaded outsider.

'Uncle, what are you doing here?' asked Urva, panting. 'You know that you aren't supposed to be anywhere near the Charna ceremony venue.'

'I am… I am sorry,' muttered Basantha with an expression of a thief meeting a soldier in the street. 'I was just anxious, you know, I am the first host of the ceremony. I just thought I would take a walk. … I am going back now. … didn't mean to intrude…'

Having watched his uncle turn back and stride away several steps, Urva returned to the Charna ceremony venue.

'Who was it? What was his intent coming over here?' asked Baba, looking slightly worried.

'My uncle Basantha,' replied Urva, approaching the oil bottle he had left on the ground. 'He wasn't in his senses.

Sleepwalking, perhaps.'

Baba didn't say anything. He quietly poured oil into a clay lamp.

'I am not sure, Baba,' said Urva, stopping short of resuming his part of the ritual. 'But there was something strange about him. He said he was taking a stroll to reduce anxiety. Perhaps, he was in his senses and knew what he was doing. Had he been someone else, I would have surely believed that he had the wrong intentions.'

'Are you sure he was Basantha?'

'Yes, Baba. It's not so dark that I could have mistaken him for someone else. I saw his face perfectly.'

Baba responded with silence, an enlightening silence.

'Oh God!' exclaimed Urva as the realization hit him like a jet of icy cold water. 'Could that be someone else in his body?'

'Yes, an Asurrah, I guess,' replied Baba speeding up the rituals which were aimed precisely at protecting the venue from the cursed souls—the Surrahs and the Asurrahs.

'It's creepy! An Asurrah hijacked the body of Uncle Basantha and walked it all the way here,' muttered Urva.

Baba let out a giggle, attempting to drown out Urva's words. He knew that talking about Asurrahs at that hour was like inviting them for supper. Leaving Urva's curious mind bubbling with thoughts on this subject was even more dangerous.

'If you want to know how they operate, wait for the Charna ceremony to begin, Urva,' said Baba, trying to sound casual. Giving importance to the subject would mean giving importance to the cursed souls he was building a shield against. 'Lord Hanuman will tell us about them first thing in the morning.'

'I have always wanted to know about them, Baba. If there are cursed souls which can use my body when my soul is away, i.e., when my body is asleep, I must be aware of them and their ways of doing what they do,' said Urva.

Baba wished he could tell Urva that the Surrahs and Asurrahs can carry out their deeds even when the body is wide awake right in the presence of the resident soul. Of all humans, the Mahtangs are the least affected by them.

When there were no empty lamps left to be filled on the boundary, Baba found an easy way to end the conversation.

'Urva, go and fill those four lamps outside the boundary, I will take care of those in the centre,' said Baba. 'And yes, those four need to be lighted right away, unlike these 164 on the periphery.'

Thankfully, Urva's curiosity now found a new subject to cling to: What was the secret ingredient of the mysterious oil? Why was it kept a secret?

He knew that it burned to emit a mysterious light that could uncover the Surrahs and Asurrahs. The four lamps were being lighted to keep the cursed souls away from the ceremony grounds; otherwise they could use a human body to barge in. They had already made an attempt through Basantha's body.

After circling around and filling the four lamps set in different directions, just when he was about to light the first lamp, Urva saw his uncle Basantha once again approaching the venue.

'Baba,' he shouted to apprise his elder companion of the situation. This time Basantha had reached much nearer before being noticed.

'Just light the lamp,' instructed Baba, pausing the rituals to monitor the situation.

Urva followed the command without any delay. The lighted lamp bathed him in a mysterious dark red light. He had expected it to do instant magic but it didn't so much as slow Basantha's pace.

'Baba, it's ineffective,' he said, turning to look from Basantha to Baba. He sensed a giant red bird flutter past his ears as he turned around. He figured it was an Asurrah and that the mysterious dark red light was revealing all the cursed souls present in the vicinity. He dashed back inside the boundary of the ceremony venue.

Baba was so assured of the power of the mysterious light that he had resumed his work.

'Baba, it's not working. He is approaching fast,' he shouted.

Baba didn't bother to respond to the impatience of a young man. He continued doing what he was doing. The light of the lamp worked when it was supposed to work. When the rays reached Basantha's eyes, his soul returned to his body and the Asurrah flew out of it. Urva saw Basantha squat and then lie down peacefully on the ground. The red bird-like figure flew towards the lamp, rose up and disappeared. He rushed to help his uncle.

'How come... why did I come here?' blabbered Basantha, sitting up straight.

'Everything is alright, uncle. No harm is done. You may

go back home,' said Urva, placing a hand on Basantha's shoulder.

The expression of mingled guilt and shame painted Basantha's face red. He stood up slowly, staggered as he turned on his way back home, and then found his pace.

Minutes later Urva and Baba completed the rituals and strode towards the hamlet.

'How does this mysterious light force Asurrahs out of the body, Baba?' asked Urva.

'It's not the light but the awareness that drives away the Surrahs and Asurrahs,' replied Baba. 'The moment you so much as suspect the presence of the cursed souls in your body, they tend to abandon it. In the case of Basantha, the mysterious light triggered this awareness. These cursed souls stay in your body only while your soul remains ignorant of their presence.'

Baba had revealed a big Mahtang community secret which Urva's otherwise sharp mind failed to register. Baba had indirectly told him that the mysterious oil whose ingredients are kept secret had no powers of its own. When the unique light emitted by the oil is seen by Mahtangs, it triggers an alert in their minds: 'Watch out for the cursed souls'. This alert generates awareness in the soul and this awareness is what forces them away. It is like a village watchman who roams around the village whistling. The whistle stops villagers from falling into deep sleep and triggers an alert in their minds: 'Watch out for thieves.'

'It's so creepy, Baba! An outsider soul can get hold of my body and do whatever it wants to do with it,' said Urva. He was familiar with the cursed souls as a concept but seeing them in action, seeing them trying to sabotage the holy ceremony through the body of his own uncle Basantha, had freaked him out.

'Your soul is as much an outsider as they are,' said Baba, scanning Urva's face with his sharp and experienced gaze for any abnormality. The tone of Urva's voice gave rise to the suspicion that an Asurrah might have got hold of his intellect. Once Baba was sure that nothing was wrong, he added, 'When a soul thinks it owns the body, it is ignorant. And ignorance, as I said, is the invitation for the cursed souls. The body your soul calls its own would continue to exist even if your soul left it and some other compatible soul took it over. It is not confirmed that your soul entered your present body right at its birth nor is it assured that you will remain in it until its death.'

Urva slept with thoughts of Surrahs and Asurrahs and encountered confusing and scary scenes in his dreams.

The Charna ceremony started two hours before dawn as scheduled.

The elder Mahtangs who had had the opportunity to receive the supreme knowledge during last visit of their immortal Guru about 41 years ago, also known as Brahmans, entered the venue first. This group was led by Baba and Mata. They chanted hymns that spoke about the eternal Mahtang tradition and about the transfer of responsibilities from one generation to another.

Urva and Urmi, the future leaders of the tribe, were then duly invited inside the venue. They were tasked with lighting the 164 lamps on the periphery of the venue under the guidance of the elders. Before the task began, they had to be warned about the creepy body-less beings that were swarming around the place.

'Are you aware that you are not a body? You *have* a body,' chorused the elder Mahtangs.

'Yes, we are. Yes, we are,' sang Urmi and Urva.

'Are you aware that you are not a mind? You *have* a mind.'

'Yes, we are. Yes, we are.'

'Are you aware that your existence has many levels, like body, mind, intellect, Samskara? And you are none of those. Are you aware that you are a soul?'

'Yes, we are. Yes, we are.'

'Are you aware of the cursed souls of the Surrah category and the Asurrah category?'

'Yes, we are. Yes, we are.'

'This is a big ceremony for us. Positive emotions are overflowing. The Surrahs, the body-less beings who relish positive flavours of human life, have gathered here in large numbers and they will try to sneak into bodies present here to taste the positive emotions. We have to be aware of them. Are you?'

'Yes, we are. Yes, we are.'

'Wherever there are positive emotions, negative emotions naturally occur. The Asurrahs, the body-less beings who relish negative flavours of human life, have gathered here in large numbers to execute their plans. They will try to creep into bodies present here and create negativities. We must stay aware of them. Are you?'

'Yes, we are. Yes, we are.'

They proceeded to light the 164 lamps on the periphery.

The cursed souls   151

The dark red light intensified with each lamp they lighted. By the time they finished their task, it had taken shape of a dark red wall around the venue. They thought they had landed inside a dark cave. They were aware that it wasn't a real wall; it was a cluster of Asurrahs swarming around and attempting to barge in.

The elder Mahtangs moved to the centre of the venue and summoned fire at the altar by lighting the pile of wood sticks of different kinds. Oblations of a sacred fluid resulted in white fragrant smoke which rose to form a surreal white dome atop the wall that had conjured a short while ago. They were aware that it wasn't a real dome; it was a cluster of Surrahs waiting for an opportunity to do what they do.

There was a writhing movement in every inch of this enclosure, the holy hemisphere as Mahtangs call it, which made it look surreal.

The elder Mahtangs along with Urva and Urmi stood up around the altar with their hands folded, eyes closed, and heads bowed, facing the seat installed for the immortal Lord Hanuman. They sang hymns that described the age-old relationship of their tribe with their immortal Guru. They submitted with all humility that they had protected their culture despite all odds.

They knew that Lord Hanuman had appeared before them when they heard His divine voice echoing in the holy hemisphere. It said, 'Open your eyes, my beloved disciples.'

They opened their eyes and lowered their bodies for prostration. They lost the sense of time. Nobody could tell how much time they had been lying stretched out on the ground, or were they even there? When the sense of time resurfaced, they thought their old bodies had melted like dirty lumps of snow; all the impurities had been washed away and now they stood perceiving the world through new, fresh human bodies.

Once Lord Hanuman took His seat, Baba instructed Urva to escort the host of the first session of the ceremony, Basantha, into the holy hemisphere. Basantha took his position. Then, rest of the Mahtangs were asked to enter the venue. The task of warning them about the presence of the cursed souls was given to Urva and Urmi. They chanted the appropriate hymns, and their audience replied with the chants of 'Yes, we are. Yes, we are.'

The talks with the immortal Guru started with a query from Urva.

'Deva, I am not sure if it's my soul speaking or some alien soul,' said Urva with a confused expressions on his face. 'Please tell us in detail about the ways and means employed by the alien souls to possess our bodies. I am curious in particular about the cursed souls.'

Urva sat down in his place and joined his fellow Mahtangs in listening to the talk of the immortal Lord Hanuman on the subject:

I observed an incident yesterday night in a devotee's house. His name is Ashok. He was having dinner. Suddenly his soul got replaced by an alien soul. His wife was looking at him from right across the dining table. She didn't notice any change in him until he asked for some pickle.

'But you hate pickle,' she said in surprise.

'So what, dear? I just feel like eating it today. Do we have it in the house?' asked Ashok.

'Yeah, sure,' said his wife, and went to the kitchen to bring pickle.

By the time she returned, Ashok's soul had returned to his body and the alien soul had ejected.

'Here, pickle,' said his wife as she scooped some out of the jar.

Ashok's soul consulted his own body-mind for a brief moment, 'Had I asked for pickle?'

Since the body-mind had the memory of asking for pickle, they replied in the affirmative. The soul didn't suspect anything strange. Ashok happily relished the pickle even though it wasn't his own desire; it was a desire planted by an alien soul.

Usually, the alien souls fully adapt to the character of the body-mind they encroach upon. In that case, the native souls have no reason to suspect anything. Even if the alien souls brought their minor characteristics into the bodies they occupy, the native souls disregard, justify and approve the minor change as a gradual, obvious change in their own nature. Ashok's soul is a case in point. It considered the planted desire as its own.

Such exchanges of souls are a norm. I also facilitate such exchanges to save devotees from trouble. Yesterday, Urmi's soul was exchanged with the soul of an old man called Ramnarayana. Except for some wise elders like Baba, none of you noticed any change in her. Such exchanges are therefore not harmful. They are rather beneficial for both the native souls and the alien souls if such exchanges are facilitated by the gods.

The problem arises when the alien souls try to impose

their characteristics on the bodies they seize control of. The cursed souls—the Surrahs and Asurrahs—are the most notorious at that.

Ordinary souls stay attached to a body so much that they feel they own it. They experience the positives and negatives of life through a single body. Only when the body becomes useless do they switch to a new one—they get a new birth.

Cursed souls, on the other hand, follow a different course: Surrahs crave only the positives of life and Asurrahs crave only negatives. They keep wandering from one body to another to enjoy their preferences. They don't stay put in a single body for long.

Fear, anger, sadness, disgust, shock, worry, and apathy are some of the major negative flavours in a human life. Imagine there is an Asurrah. It finds a person who is fearful. It will enter his body and savour fear. It will try to keep him fearful as long as possible, but when the fear is no longer there, it will abandon his body. It will then search for some other target. Suppose it found a sad person. It will enter her body and savour sadness and prolong it if possible. When she is no longer sad, it will vacate her body. It will proceed on to find new targets who are fearful, angry, sad, disgusted, shocked, worried, apathetic to others, etc.

Joy, trust, hope, amazement, and sympathy are some of the major positive flavours in a human life. Surrahs keep a lookout for people who are going through such positives and enter their body-minds to savour and prolong what they crave most—the positive flavours of human life.

People whose body-minds have once been used by the cursed souls become susceptible to them because the latter identify the former as potential targets and try to linger around them for further opportunities. They even create opportunities for themselves.

It is completely human to be sad, and there is no harm if an Asurrah enters your body to savour the sadness. The harm is when the Asurrah tries to make you perennially sad. It plants negative thoughts in your mind so that you start seeing problems where there are none.

It is completely human to trust somebody, and there is no harm if a Surrah enters your body to savour the feeling of trust. The harm is when the Surrah tries to convert your trust into a blind trust. It plants positive thoughts in your mind so that you start trusting even your enemies.

It is completely human to be angry, and there is no harm if an Asurrah relishes anger through your body. The harm is when it gets hold of you, plants thoughts in your mind, and uses anger as an ingredient to create more negatives.

It is completely human to eat delicious sweets, and there is no harm if a Surrah enters your body and savours the pleasure along with you. The harm is when it tries to a convert one-time pleasure into an addiction.

It is completely human to believe in something staunchly. The harm is when Asurrahs get hold of your mind, make you blind and disrespectful of others' beliefs and create hatred and relish it.

There are three ways to get rid of the cursed souls depending on their types: Beware, Refuse, and Pray.

Some of them are like sneaky thieves who flee as soon as their victim wakes up. The knowledge I am giving you about their nature will sound an alarm when they sneak into your body-mind. If sadness lingers in you, for instance, you will figure out that Asurrahs have barged in. This realization itself is enough to shake them out of your body-mind.

You also need to beware of the cursed souls that might have seized control of not your body-mind but that of people you interact with. For example, if your friend constantly complains about something, beware that he or she may be under the control of Asurrahs. This awareness itself is enough to keep you insulated, but the lack thereof may result in those Asurrahs seizing control of you as well. If your friend is addicted to something, beware of the Surrahs that are possibly controlling him. This awareness itself is enough to keep you insulated from him and the addiction.

So, to get rid of the cursed souls of thief type, just beware.

Some of the Surrahs and Asurrahs are like a conman. They fool you into giving control to them. Suppose, you hate dogs; continual hatred against anything is a sign of the presence of Asurrahs in your body-mind. They have coloured your world with their brush so that you come across incidents that justify your hatred. You hear news of dogs mauling humans. You see victims of dog bites dying a horrible death. Your hatred may increase to the point that you make it your mission to kill and harm dogs.

The external world is limitless. You see only a limited version of it, and if you give control of your mind to the Asurrahs they will show you what serves them best. They will show you everything that might bring the negative flavours in your life that they crave for. They will fool you into believing that what they show you is the complete world. Hatred will be followed by anger, fear, disgust, worry, shock, apathy and so on. More and more Asurrahs will nest in your body-mind and knock your soul out of business. You will believe them to be your soul while your soul will be huddled in a dark corner of ignorance.

To get rid of them, you need to refuse to believe in your worldview. You must refuse to believe that what you see is the only reality. Even if everything you perceive and everyone you know validates your worldview, just refuse it. It is like saying 'no' to a swindler who sounds convincing to you in every way. Simply saying 'no' a couple of times will irritate them and they will either flee quietly or show their true colours.

Suppose, you love dogs; you shower your compassion and kindness on them. Some Surrahs have, of course, sneaked into your body-mind to relish these positive flavours. They may even seize control of you and start manufacturing more and more reasons for you to be compassionate and kind to dogs. What is wrong in that, you ask? The enlightened ones also live a life full of compassion.

The problem is, if you have lost control of your body-mind to Surrahs, you have rendered yourself susceptible to Asurrahs too. No doubt Surrahs will bring positives into your life, but Asurrahs, who outnumber Surrahs in this world, will try to bring negative flavours.

The Surrahs who were the original intruders in your body-mind might form a coalition with Asurrahs on a common agenda. Asurrahs, by way of planting thoughts, will create problems in your life, thereby slipping you into sadness, anger, fear and other negatives. You may, for instance, develop misunderstandings with your family, friends, and society at large. It will help Surrahs further their agenda and make you believe that only dogs are your true companions. On the one hand, you will be compassionate toward dogs and on the other hand, you will be angry, sad, fearful, apathetic, disgusted, and worried for or because of other creatures, including your fellow human beings.

The solution, again, is to refuse to believe what you are made to believe by the cursed souls. They will flee and things will start getting back to normal in your life.

Even nastier than the thief type and conman type are the goon type of the cursed souls. They openly exercise their powers on your body-mind. Take an example from the life of Basantha. He was once climbing a tricky branch of a tree. It became trickier when he saw a nest set on it. He tried to carefully creep forward but ended up placing one of his feet in the nest and breaking the eggs laid therein. His heart was filled with regret and pain for next couple of days and Asurrahs relished it. How did his leg stretch to the nest despite his efforts to the contrary? Because of an Asurrah that saw an opportunity there and seized control of his body to commit the deed.

Once the cursed souls accomplish one deed, they get emboldened and try to commit an even bigger deed. That Asurrah managed to commit one more evil deed a few days later, this time seizing control of not only Basantha's body but also his mind. He was collecting honey and saw a nest causing a hindrance. He, this time mindfully, kicked down the nest, not realizing that there were eggs inside it. He later regretted it and blamed himself, although it was an Asurrah who had done it by capturing his body and mind.

Not long after that, the same Asurrah seized control

of not only his body and mind but also his intellect and ideology. Baba had asked him to bring a feather of a blue sparrow. When he failed to find a fallen feather, he decided to kill a sparrow. A Mahtang killing a bird to obtain a feather! And he didn't even regret it because his ideology along with his ability to tell good from bad had been held hostage by the Asurrah. He later staunchly argued with Baba on this subject. His argument was that the bird had to die one day anyway. The Asurrah savoured every drop of trouble that brewed between two Mahtangs that day.

Prayer has the power to free you from all three types of cursed souls. You should pray at the beginning of a time period: a day, a week, a fortnight, a month, a year. Let me tell you how to perform a daily prayer.

At the end of a day, get something to offer to your deity. It can be leaves, flowers, fruits or anything procured with love and faith. The next day in the morning, sit quietly before your deity and make your offerings one by one. With each item you offer, the incidents you went through during the previous day will flash in your mind. Surrender them all to your deity. If something made you sad during the previous day, just surrender it to your deity. If something gave you joy during the previous day, just surrender it to your deity. Whether life gave you a positive flavour or a negative one, just surrender it to your deity. When you keep neither negatives nor positives with you, Asurrahs or Surrahs are left with no motivation to capture your body-mind. The prayer will purify your soul, and you will be able to experience the new day without any interference of the cursed souls. You can do prayers similarly at the beginning of a new week, a new fortnight, a new month and so on.

An ordinary soul, as you know, passes through positives and negatives, lives one life after another, keeps rolling in the cycle of birth and death until it gets liberation, the Moksha. What if it didn't get Moksha even after living through ages? Does it stay trapped in the Human World for infinity? Or to put it another way, does your soul have infinite time here in the Human World? No. Not only your body's but also your soul's time here is limited.

This world is like a road and mortal bodies are like chariots running on it. Your soul came here to enjoy a ride but ended up stuck on what seems like a never-ending road. The road indeed is never ending but you don't have a pass to stay here forever. If a chariot (mortal body) broke, you could hop onto another one. But this can't go on for infinity.

You see, more and more souls are descending on this road to enjoy the ride. There comes a time when the road becomes so congested that it gets annihilated along with the chariots. The stuck souls on the right side (positive side) of the road get pushed to the right and become Surrahs. Those on the left side (negative side) get pushed to the left and become Asurrahs. The road emerges again, fresh and new, but the old passes are not valid on it. The Surrahs and Asurrahs therefore become illegal riders. They stealthily or forcefully try to occupy the new chariots.

Speaking off the road-chariot analogy, you don't have infinite time here in this world. You must get Moksha before the world annihilates. If you don't, you will either become a Surrah or an Asurrah and wander in the new world that will emerge after annihilation.

You are blessed that my words are reaching you. They will show you the way out.